Cat's Eyes

Cat's Eyes

By
Lee Jordan

NAL BOOKS
NEW AMERICAN LIBRARY
TIMES MIRROR
NEW YORK AND SCARBOROUGH, ONTARIO

Publisher's Note

This novel is a work of fiction. Names, characters, places, and incidents are either the product of the author's imagination or are used fictitiously, and any resemblance to actual persons, living or dead, events, or locales is entirely coincidental.

Cat's Eyes

1

First the tapping.

It came above the noise of the wind and the rain. A tapping.
At the window.

Then the man's face.

Rain pouring down his head mixing with the blood; dark holes
where his eyes should have been; white fingers pressed against
the glass.

Sometimes it was Bill's face; sometimes Charlie's.

Then came the scream. She seemed to stand outside herself
and watch herself screaming.

Always the tapping. Tap . . . tap . . .

Then the face, then the scream.

Then the cat.

It sat in the middle of the shining black road: huge, lit from
behind like some giant monolith.

Then the crash . . .

2

Rachel Chater could feel the scream in her throat as she swam up through the layers of sleep and broke into wakefulness. Her mouth was open but no sound came; the scream had been silent, like her sleep. She opened her eyes and reached for Bill, but he was not there.

For a second, she felt panic—then she remembered: Bill was on his way to California and she was here, in the house tucked into the Sussex Downs, with her baby daughter Sophie, the girl Penny, and Nurse Griffin for company.

Her knee was aching and the dream was still vivid in her mind, its elements separating into stages, each stage remorselessly following the last, gathering speed as it had in reality, until the final blackout.

She told herself that now it *was* only a dream and fought the tension in her body. She remembered the yoga exercise for relaxing: place the thumbs against the first fingers to make a circle and let them rest by your sides; allow yourself to relax, concentrate on each muscle, let the muscles become jelly. Slowly, she felt her body soften. The throb in her right knee became worse but the dream began to disappear as though down the small end of a telescope, until finally it was gone, and only the desolation and loneliness remained. The day stretched ahead of her and she began to wonder how on earth she would fill it—and all the other days—until Bill came home.

Home? Hell, *this* wasn't home! She pushed back the blankets and dragged herself painfully from the bed. Her injured knee had stiffened and she put her weight on it gingerly. It had let her down several times when she had tested it in the hospital and she had ended in a heap on the floor. But the doctors had said she must walk, so each time she had grimly hauled herself up and tried again. Now she hobbled to the window and drew back the curtains.

It was early autumn, a damp, gray morning, and she looked out over the dripping landscape, which was uninterrupted by any other sign of human habitation.

Suddenly she yearned for the sea, real sea, the Pacific off Santa Monica; the great swells coming into the Monterey Peninsula; even the greeny slicks off Nantucket. She had always thought of the sea as a healer. When she had worked in New York and winter had lingered, she had looked forward to the cold salt water of early summer to wash away her problems, both physical and mental. She supposed that the same efficacy, if there was any, was to be found in salt water wherever it was, but it did not feel the same. She had swum once in the English Channel and had found the water cold and soupy, and the pebbles had hurt her feet. She wanted the seas she knew. Home.

But whatever her yearnings, this *was* home now, this gray countryside, this rambling house set in the middle of what had once been England's Great Forest, with its trees and shadows and dark, often impenetrable thickets. The house was gloomy, too. There were rooms that needed electric light even on the sunniest days, and long, shadowy corridors that twisted and turned into the heart of the house. The plaster on some of the ceilings was cracked, and sometimes she lay in bed imagining the cracks widening silently, like living things.

It was at once a silent and a noisy house. When she was in it by herself during the day the walls were too thick, the windows too small to allow the friendly sounds of birdsong and wind in the trees to penetrate. Occasionally in the beginning she had been driven to create her own noise, deliberately walking heavily on the wooden floors, singing, whistling, even talking to herself. But at night the house moved, its old wood expanding and contracting, grating and groaning as though it, too, were alive.

She had never suffered from claustrophobia in California. In England, since her accident, everything seemed to close in on her; the shadowy house with its leaded windowpanes; the trees around it, cutting off light and space; the lowering skies, too often dripping with rain; the countryside itself, with its small fields jealously protected by high hedges in which brambles, oak, deadly nightshade, beech, and thorn twisted inextricably; the thatched cottages whose doors always seemed closed; the great stone walls hiding houses with windows like opaque blind eyes.

When Bill was with her she could ignore her fanciful apprehensions, but now, alone, she was swept by homesickness, not only for the sea, but for California's warmth and color, for space, mountains, deserts, forests, and great cloudless skies.

There was a knock on the door and Miss Griffin came in. Rachel had met her for the first time on her return from the hospital three days before, and did not care for her. Neither, she knew instinctively, did the woman like her. Bill had found her and told Rachel about her the first time he had come to see her in the hospital after the accident, when she was still muzzy and in shock, scarcely aware of the conversation.

"We're incredibly lucky," he had said. "She's a retired nurse who lives in Chichester. Not a thing of beauty and charm, but she seems efficient and likes babies. She wouldn't commit herself, but I think she'll stay as long as we need her."

Later, Rachel realized he had not exaggerated their good fortune. Reliable children's nurses were few and far between. They had been living in Lexton for such a short time that they had had no friends who might have cared for Sophie. Bill's parents were dead—as were her own—and he had no close relatives.

As she turned from the window the woman said, "I've put Sophie to bed. It's nearly eleven, Mrs. Chater. Is there anything I can do for you?" Her tone was cold.

"Not a thing, thanks. I guess I'll go and see Sophie as soon as I'm dressed."

"I would suggest you left it for a while. I had trouble getting her to sleep."

As she turned and closed the door behind her with a snap, Rachel made a face at the rigid back. She had first set eyes on Miss Griffin—or Nurse Griffin, as she liked to be called—as she had limped up the steps to the front door, with Bill's arm around her waist supporting her. It was an immense effort, and even the short drive from the hospital had tired her.

As she dressed, she remembered how she had looked forward to her return, waiting in her private hospital room for Bill to collect her. For the first time she had thought with affection of the gaunt, angular house he had bought before her arrival from America.

The first jolt to her happiness had occurred when the surgeon had visited her. He was a sleek man running to plumpness and premature baldness. As befitted his membership in the private side of British medicine, he wore a dark jacket and striped trousers, a shirt of dark blue Bengal stripes and white collar; as a concession to youth, he wore a mauve silk tie.

He was pleasant enough, she thought, but his ponderous manner gave an impression of middle age, though he could not have been more than thirty-six.

She had been sitting on her bed when he arrived.

"Today's the day," he had said. "How long have we had you now?"

"Three weeks."

"A long time to be away from home, especially when you have a small baby." As he talked he began to examine her knee. "Does that hurt?"

"A little."

"Can you bend it? Good. What's her name?"

"Sophie." He had asked her this twice before.

"I imagine your husband will be glad to see you back. Straighten it. A writer, isn't he? Tell me, does he . . . Can you lift it a little bit more? That's better. Does he keep regular hours or does he write when the inspiration comes over him?"

It was one of a stock set of questions that people asked. If they had not heard of Bill they said, "Does he write under his own name?" If they *had* heard of him, they said, "Afraid I don't get time to read much." Sometimes they said, "Should I have read anything of his?"

"He goes to work every morning after breakfast, like anyone else," Rachel said. "He has a room in the garden where he's undisturbed."

"Yes, well, that's doing very nicely." He closed her dressing gown primly. "There's always going to be a little stiffness. I think you must prepare yourself for that."

They talked for a while about exercises and finally he said, "How do you feel about driving again?"

She was about to say she felt terrified, but stopped herself. It was too emotional a word: a writer's word. He might take her literally, as he took most things, and so she said, "Apprehensive, I guess,"

"You won't be able to do much for a while, anyway. The knee won't stand the strain, especially if you have to brake suddenly."

"It won't matter. My husband loves driving."

"Your house is rather isolated, isn't it?"

"I suppose so."

When she had first arrived from America she had been reminded of the countryside between Paso Robles and the sea in central California. It was the same type of landscape, of folding hills and winding roads, leading she never knew where, to cutoff places and secret valleys. But soon she had discovered that the Sussex Downs had a character entirely their own and she never ceased to be amazed that in overcrowded England there was so much land that still appeared to be as empty as it must have been in the days, centuries ago, when forest had covered much of the island. There were still so many trees. She had never seen such woods. They rose out of the bottom land and towered up from the sides of the Downs, great hardwoods: beech and ash and oak, magnificent umbrellas of green in summer, stark and witchlike in winter. And then there were wide, empty views from the grassed tops of the Downs, where a chalky hiker's track wound over the hilltops for miles.

Since her arrival, she had come to regard the Downs as an escape when the house threatened to close in on her. If Bill was busy, she would drive up one of the narrow roads that led to the top, park the car and walk, able to see to east or west over the valleys. She liked it best on clear days in autumn and winter when she could look into the distance, or even on days when wind from the north swept over the Downs and she had to lean into it, cleansing herself as she had in the sea. That was when England's gentle climate was transformed into *weather* and she loved its challenge.

She became aware that the surgeon was still talking: "I've been out your way. Always get lost. Real Indian country." He smiled at his little joke, then stood up. "Good luck, Mrs. Chater."

"Thank you."

At the door, he had turned. "It was sad about Leech," he said. She looked at him, startled. He had never mentioned Charlie before. "I knew him. His father was a jobbing gardener. He worked for my mother for years. In the school holidays he used to bring Charlie round from job to job. We played together as children." He was staring at her. "The inquest report said he had been working for you."

"Yes."

"He was always good with his hands."

Especially where his hands weren't wanted, she thought bitterly. She did not want to discuss Charlie Leech, nor what had happened. But the doctor had stood there while a little silence grew. Then he said, "It's unfortunate your husband wasn't home."

When he had gone she found that her heart was beating rapidly. Why had he mentioned Charlie? What was he implying? Did he think that she and Charlie . . . ? God, could he be thinking that she and Charlie had been having a squalid little affair while her husband was away? Is that what others would be thinking? Did Bill think that? She rejected the idea as preposterous, but elements of it remained. It had not occurred to her before.

And then, as she waited for Bill, the dream had suddenly become visible on her inner eye in chiaroscuro: first, the tapping . . . She felt herself growing cold as she realized that she had dreamed the same dream at least three times. The tapping, the face, and, most terrifying of all, the cat.

She told herself, as she had told herself since, that the events that had set off the dream were in the past. She remembered, from a course in classical history she had taken in California, Polybius' pragmatic view of history and his thesis that what one learns from the past shapes one's future behavior. But there was nothing in the past, at least in the past that inspired the dream, from which she could learn. The dream was simply a dream, reality coming to the surface of her mind in sleep, for everything about the dream had once been real, and she did not want to remember it. But it was not the past but the future that was bothering her, and she knew at least one of the reasons: one day, when she was home, she would have to see Mrs. Leech, Charlie's widow. Bill had already visited her, given her money. Rachel had written saying how desperately sorry she was to have been the unwitting cause of Charlie's death. But she would have to see her. There was no escaping it.

Then Bill had arrived and the joy of seeing him had swept away the horrors. Temporarily.

At first she had enjoyed the drive home. They passed a pub called the Fox and Grapes, where they had sometimes lunched, and a few minutes later turned off the main road and began to wind up into the folded, closed, and secretive heart of the Downs, along a lane that ran between high thorn hedges. There were objects she recognized: a mailbox, a red telephone booth standing isolated in the middle of nowhere, a flint farmhouse, hayricks that she had seen building at the end of the previous summer, chicken houses, calf pens, and everywhere trees. They passed into the parish of Lexton itself and all these things had coalesced into *her* landscape, of which, willy-nilly, she was a part.

Lexton lay in a valley surrounded by woods that seemed to cut it off from the mainstream of Sussex life. It had no center in the manner of picturesque English postcard villages with their streams and ponds and rows of thatched cottages. It had a shop which combined its mercantile function with that of sub–post office; a pub; a harness-maker who now made wallets and belts as often as he mended bridles and stirrup leathers; a blacksmith who no longer shod horses but made ornamental ironwork; a book bindery; and a bungalow advertising cream teas. But all were separated from each other by fields and copses; even the church stood alone.

Once she had flown over the Downs in a helicopter with Bill. "That's where we live," he had shouted, pointing. "There's the house." She had looked down and had hardly been able to detect the break in the trees that was their three acres of paddock and garden. Everywhere below seemed to be unbroken green.

It was only later, once she had begun, like a good immigrant, to read about her new land, that she had found they were living in what remained of the Great Forest, that dark and frightening area which had stretched along the south coast of Britain in ancient times, a place of superstition and dread, harboring only charcoal-burners, iron-workers, and fugitives. It had once formed part of the Kingdom of the South Saxons, and in her reading she had come across people with names like Ella and Cissa, Aethelwald and Ceadwalla, who had lived and fought on the edge of the Great Forest. Sometimes, on a dull day, looking out of the drawing-room window across the paddock at the beech trees with their screaming rookeries, she was able to visualize the mile upon mile of gloomy forest, with only a pinpoint of light to show where the iron-worker had his forge.

They had come to a crossroads and Bill turned right. One lane looked very much like another and she was still not completely familiar with the sprawling parish, which was said to have more than eighty miles of narrow, hedged roadway. Half hidden by blackberries, she had seen the sign that said Pickaxe Lane and had felt sick. This was the way she had driven Charlie home, this was where the accident had happened. They had come to the top of a rise. There was the tree she had hit. Momentarily her courage had failed her and she had closed her eyes, not wanting to look at it, afraid of the picture it would bring to her mind. Then she had thought, Don't be so silly, it's only a tree. As they drew level with it, she had forced herself to look for damage. She was not sure what to expect: a mass of torn foliage, smashed branches. But there had been hardly anything to see: a single rip in the bark, a couple of sappy bruises where someone might have hit it with a large hammer; that was all. Then suddenly she had been thrown forward as Bill braked.

"My Christ!" he said. "What's that?"

She had followed his glance. At first she could see nothing except a black boulder half hidden by the tall grass. When the boulder moved, she realized that it was an animal. It had stood for a moment, watching them, then disappeared into the hedgerow.

"I've never seen a cat as big as that," he said. "Never."

Rachel knew it was the cat from her dream. The monolith. The cat that had caused Charlie Leech's death; the cat that had caused her to spend the past three weeks in the hospital with a smashed knee. It was *the* cat.

She turned, wanting to tell Bill, wanting to share her terror, needing his comfort. But before she could speak he said, with unusual vehemence, "I *hate* cats!"

Surprised, she had said, "Do you? I didn't know that."

He had smiled at her. "You weren't thinking of getting one, were you?"

"After what happened to me? God, no!"

She had not said anything else about the cat, but as they drove on she sat stiffly, seeing the great black shape in her mind's eye, too absorbed in her thoughts to realize that Bill, too, was silent, looking ahead through the windshield, a frown drawing his eyebrows together.

To distract herself she had said quickly, "Tell me about Sophie. You're sure she's being properly looked after by this Miss What's-her-name?"

"Griffin. She's coping very well. She doesn't say much, but she seems to be fond of Sophie. You might have to fight for your daughter's attention."

"I hope I won't have to do anything of the kind!" she said indignantly, then realized he was teasing her and laughed. "I've missed her almost as much as I've missed you. It's absurd! I never thought I'd be a possessive mom . . ."

"*Mum.* You're in England now."

". . . but there have been times when I've ached for her. Once or twice when you told me about her I hated that nurse for being with her when I wasn't."

A few minutes later the drive gates had loomed up on the left and, behind them, the steeply pitched roof of the house.

As he had turned into the drive, she saw a notice on the gate. In big black letters drawn by a felt marker were the words, "Welcome home!" She had felt tears spring to her eyes and a lump form in her throat, and had put her arm through his.

The house stood well back from the road at the end of a short, curving drive, and was almost hidden by high beech hedges. It was tall and angular, like Bill himself, but instead of his easygoing charm it had, she thought, a gauntness and a secretiveness unlike most of the other soft, yellow-stoned cottages of Sussex.

Parts of it dated from the sixteenth century, and it had been added to over the years. In Victoria's time it had been a rectory and another section had been built on, faced with gray flint. The constant additions had given it winding passages, two staircases, short corridors that seemed to lead nowhere. It was everything that Rachel's childhood homes in California had not been. There she had been used to space and sunny colors; here small, damp, musty-smelling rooms opened into other small rooms that opened into the narrow passages that sometimes ended in blank walls.

Bill had brought her straight to the house that day she had arrived from America nearly a year before, and during the drive from Heathrow to Sussex she had discovered how worried he was about her reaction to it.

"It's *not* what you've been accustomed to," he said anxiously. "Don't expect your open-plan, split-level ranch house. It's old. It has the dust of ages in the floorboards. It's been neglected—but we'll work on it. It has potential . . . anyway, there wasn't anything else at short notice at a price I could afford."

Finally she had said, laughing, "For heaven's sake, stop fussing! I'll love it. As long as we're together."

But even she had been silenced by the first sight of the house huddled behind its hedge and had needed to make a conscious effort to smile at him reassuringly as they had moved into the dark corridors. There had been a smell of damp, an atmosphere of decay and neglect, that had made her shiver.

Her first feeling had been that she could never live in such a gloomy place, but as the months had passed and she had replaced some of the heavy furniture Bill had bought with the house, she had begun to see how it could be made livable. Just before her accident, when autumn had brought an early cold snap, she had, for the first time, even begun to enjoy it. The small rooms warmed by open fires or wood stoves, the wings that could be closed off, the huge farmhouse kitchen with its solid fuel stove, had, she realized, been designed for a way of life different from that of California, a cozy, indoor life insulated from the dismal prospect outside.

There were few trees near the house. They had been cut down years before, and the three acres of grass gave the impression of being a clearing in the forest, which, in fact, it was. At the back was a paddock overgrown by grass and nettles. Once it had been an orchard, but the trees had slowly died of neglect and canker and the last of them were waiting to be cut for firewood.

As Bill had helped her out of the car the front door had opened and a woman stood in the doorway. She was short and stocky. Her hair was iron-gray and basin-cut. She wore thick pebble glasses that exaggerated the size of her eyes and gave her a hyperthyroid look. She was dressed in a flowered smock and had an air of severity and no-nonsense competence.

Rachel had smiled and held out her hand. "You must be Miss Griffin."

"Nurse Griffin. How do you do?" She had a deep, mannish voice and her speech was clipped, as though she might once have been an army officer.

As they went into the house the telephone had rung in Bill's study. "I'll get it," he said.

"It never stops ringing," Nurse Griffin had said disapprovingly. "All day long and half the night." For a moment Rachel felt that the nurse was the hostess and she a visitor in her own house. She heard Bill close his study door.

"Where's Sophie?"

"She's asleep. I wouldn't disturb her now, she hasn't been well. Nothing to worry about, but a nasty cough."

"Don't worry. I won't disturb her." She went upstairs to the baby's room.

The curtains had been closed and the central heating radiator was on. Sophie lay on her side in the crib and her little face was flushed. She had been put to bed as though she were a doll, blankets tucked up to her chin. She had clearly been struggling to free herself and had almost turned over.

Rachel bent to kiss her. Having spent most of her life in a society that did much of its living out of doors, she believed in fresh air as she believed in the sea. She believed in sunshine as a life- and health-giving force, and whenever possible she put Sophie outside in a carriage. She turned off the radiator and opened the window.

Cough or no cough, it seemed better for the child to be cool and comfortable than restless under a load of blankets in an overheated room.

She had stood by the cot, willing herself not to pick the baby up and hug her. Suddenly Sophie opened her eyes. Her face puckered as though she were about to cry, then it changed and she smiled. Rachel told herself the child knew her and felt her love almost as a physical force.

There was no need to be careful now. She pulled back the covers, lifted Sophie and kissed her. "You're growing more hair!" Sophie put up a hand and gripped her forefinger. She had been almost bald at birth and had had a touch of jaundice. Bill had called her Chairman Mao. Now her hair was growing in spiky tufts. Rachel smoothed them back, then carried her to the window and looked out at the gnarled trees in the paddock. There was a noise behind her and she turned. Nurse Griffin had opened the door.

"Mrs. Chater, the child should not be in a draft."

"I'm her mother, Nurse Griffin," Rachel said sharply. "I'm perfectly capable of looking after her."

The woman had started to speak, then tightened her mouth.

"I'll put her down when she wants to go down," Rachel said. "Is Mrs. Aske still here?" Mrs. Aske was the cleaning woman, who came in for three hours every morning.

"She has left." The tone was chilly.

"Left? You mean she doesn't come at all?"

"Her husband has taken a job in Bristol."

"I didn't know . . ."

"Mr. Chater did not want to worry you."

"When did she leave?"

"Three days ago."

"So you've been holding the fort by yourself?"

"I have." She closed the door and left mother and child together.

"Wow! That was frosty!" Rachel whispered in Sophie's ear. "Come on, let's go see your father."

Neither Rachel nor Bill knew that the cat had watched the car as it disappeared down the side of the hill, then had come out of the safety of the hedgerow and moved cautiously along the side of the road, keeping to the tall grass and the cow parsley. Nor had they noticed that the cat limped. Its left back leg had been damaged in the same accident that had caused the injury to Rachel's leg and the death of Charlie Leech. But whereas Charlie was long past caring about what damage the accident had done to him, and Rachel Chater knew that her life would go on much as it had before, the injury to the cat had been ruinous. One of the car's wheels had crushed its left back paw. It could only spring with the power of one leg, and this was a severe handicap to its hunting ability.

There was a difference between it and other cats. It was no pet, but a domestic cat that had gone wild, a feral cat.

For days it had tried to capture its usual food of rats, mice, voles, rabbits, and birds, but they were now too quick for it, and in the period immediately after the accident it had nearly starved to death.

But it was a survivor and soon learned to fight the crows for the dead squirrels and the mashed rabbits who themselves were victims of road accidents. Sometimes the crows got there first and sometimes there were no bodies lying on the black asphalt in the morning to tell of the night's carnage. On those days, the cat went hungry.

Bill had broken his news to her after lunch, when they were in the garden hut where he did most of his work. It was not much more than a shed containing a desk, reference books, a typewriter, a large easy chair, and a divan. Sophie was asleep in her room, Nurse Griffin was in the house, and for the first time Rachel had felt she could relax and enjoy being home. She lay on the divan, propped up against the cushions, resting her leg. Bill was in his swivel office chair, turning slowly from side to side. He was dressed in jeans, a plaid shirt, and moccasins. The informal clothes suited him, she thought. Looking at him with fresh eyes after being away, she had registered once more what an attractive face he had, the eyes filled with humor and warmth. He was a good-looking man, there was no doubt about that. She had only to watch the reactions of other women when he walked into a crowded room. He was nearly forty but looked younger, although, as she studied him, she could see there were new lines and his eyes looked tired. He had seemed to be preoccupied ever since they had reached home and she felt an inexplicable pang of apprehension.

"Bill, what's wrong?" she said suddenly.

He had made no attempt to prevaricate. Looking at her directly he said, "I have to go to Hollywood for at least six weeks."

She stared at him in shocked silence, unable to absorb the meaning of his words. Then she said, "You're going away? When?"

"On the twentieth."

"But that's in three days!"

She felt tears pricking her eyes. Having just come out of the hospital, was she really to be left in this gaunt, isolated house for six weeks, with only a baby and the grim-faced Nurse Griffin for company?

"I don't believe it!" she said. "You can't!"

"I'm afraid I must."

Arguments churned in her mind: she was still weak and ill after her accident . . . the house was too remote . . . they knew so few people . . . suppose Sophie became ill? . . . he had no *right* to leave her!

Her instinct was to beg him not to go, but before she cried out she realized that he looked as unhappy as she felt and managed to swallow the words.

"Darling, it couldn't have come at a worse time, but there hasn't been a damn thing I could do about it," he said. "I tried to put it off. I told them you were just out of hospital, but *you* know what they're like. They've made up their minds and nothing will change them."

"But what's it all about? And why didn't you tell me before?"

"Nothing was certain. I thought it might all fall through. It started about three days after your accident. Maxwell called from the West Coast . . ." Maxwell was his Hollywood literary agent. "He said that Franco Talini . . ."

"Who's he?"

"One of the new crop of young Italian producers. Maxwell said he was planning a remake of *Trilby*. He was putting together a package and wanted me to do the screenplay."

"*Trilby?* It's deadly. Have you read it?"

"Not for years."

"So what did you say?"

"I said I was interested. Then, typical bloody Hollywood, they started buggering me around. One minute it was on and the next it was off, he was trying to find backing, he'd found backing, he hadn't found backing. They've been on the phone a dozen times in the past week alone. Then last night Max called and said it was fixed. The contract is ready, but they want me at once or it's all off."

"What about your book? And the play you wanted to write?"

"I can't afford not to take this job." He hesitated. "I didn't want to go into this quite so soon, but I've got next year's tax assessment. We're damn nearly broke. That's why I need the screenplay."

"What about the American paperback deal on *Bird of Paradise?*" It was his latest novel, which had been published in England some months before.

"It fell through the day after you went into hospital." He smiled at her without amusement. "One way and another, it's been a fairly eventful few weeks."

She felt a wave of compunction. She had been absorbed in self-pity, anticipating her own loneliness, and had given his problems scarcely a thought. He had taken nearly a year to write *Bird of Paradise* and he'd had high hopes for it. It had sold readily enough to his hardback publishers in London and New York, but she knew that he had been counting on a paperback house liking it enough to produce a substantial dollar advance. The average hardcover novel, as he had explained, brought in barely enough money for them to live on, let alone pay the mortgage on the house. A novelist's profit was made on subsidiary rights: paperbacks, book clubs, film options, foreign sales. There were, he had added, only about two thousand authors in England able to live solely on their book earnings. She had been impressed by the fact that he was one of them.

She remembered how he had taken a telephone call from his New York agent late one evening, not long before her accident. Curled up in an armchair, she had listened unashamedly and known that there was good news when his voice had risen to a delighted shout: "That's even better than I'd hoped. When will they publish?"

There had been a pause, then he had said more quietly, "No, I won't—but I think Rachel and I might be justified in a small celebration in anticipation!"

When he had returned the telephone to rest he was smiling, his eyes bright. "Excelsior Press is interested in paperback rights to *Bird of Paradise*. Guess what they're likely to offer?"

"Ten, fifteen thousand?" she said hopefully.

"Double it! Henry says it isn't firm enough for us to buy the Rolls—but it would be in order to open a bottle of nonvintage champagne."

They'd had the champagne, but Excelsior had been taken over by a multinational, there had been staff changes, and the sale had not matured.

"Someone else will take it," she said.

He shrugged. "I can't count on a maybe. I have a wife and child to keep. I hate leaving you, my love, especially now, but I promise you I won't be away a moment longer than I have to."

"Can't Sophie and I come too?" Even as she said it she knew it was impossible. She was in no condition to travel, especially with a small baby.

He was shaking his head regretfully. "Apart from your leg and the money it would involve, I'm going to have to work closely with Talini. Max said he wants us to go to a cabin in the mountains someone's lent him so there will be no interruptions."

Tears were still threatening, but she controlled them and even smiled at him. There was hardly a tremor in her voice as she said, "Lucky you! Well, Sophie and I will have to find our own amusement. I'll be able to catch up on the typing, anyway. Have you much of the book for me?"

He shook his head. "Not this time," he said. "I'm taking the manuscript with me. New system: I want you to come at it fresh when it's finished. I'll have it typed in Los Angeles, then bring back the finished copy."

"How much have you done?"

"Nearly eighty pages."

"Hey, you've been working! You hadn't even started it when I went into the hospital."

"All day and half the night, without you to distract me. Not that I wouldn't rather be distracted. But the sooner it's finished, the sooner we get the advance."

Knowing now what had caused the deep lines around his eyes and the papery look of his skin, her heart went out to him. He was a strange mixture. On the surface he appeared confident, easygoing, relaxed. Underneath he was gentle and anxious and worried and conscientious, and the signs of strain were beginning to show. But that was a hazard of his type of work, never knowing from one year to the next how much he was going to earn—or how little. And before they even started to live he had to pay a regular amount into a bank account for his first wife, Sally, who had disappeared from his life, apparently, long before Rachel had met him.

She knew little about his first marriage, for beyond telling her early in their acquaintance that he *had* been married, he barely mentioned Sally. At first she had been curious, but as he was obviously reluctant to discuss it, she had never asked questions. From the little he said, she had gained the impression that the marriage had not been happy. She did not even know whether the sums he paid out were court-awarded alimony or a private arrangement. In any case, she did not resent them, as Sally was obviously never going to intrude on their lives. As the months passed, Rachel had almost forgotten her existence.

"At least tell me what the book's about," she said.

Again he shook his head and she caught a curiously uncomfortable movement of his eyes. "It's to be a surprise. I really do want your unbiased opinion on this one."

She knew that her most valuable function in his work was her ability to read a completed manuscript with a trained eye and give her opinion not only as a reader, but as a professional who was involved in the writing business herself. She dismissed her momentary puzzlement.

"Okay. It'll be something else to look forward to when you come back," she said. "Will you have a chance to do any work on it while you're in L.A.?"

"I hope so. Between sessions with Talini. I'm using this . . ." He picked up a battery-operated, hand-held dictating machine from the desk. "It wasn't easy to dictate at first, but I've been getting better at it and I've done nearly twenty thousand words in less than a week. Some of it has already been typed at an agency in Chichester. Those are the tapes." He pointed to a pile of cassettes on a shelf.

He showed her how it worked, the start-and-stop button, the rewind of the tiny tape cassette that fitted snugly into the side. "I can lie down or walk around. I can dicate anywhere."

He was fiddling with the machine, flicking it on and off, and she had the impression that he would like to get back to work.

She had eased herself off the divan. By the time she had limped past the window he was already hunched over his desk, dictating machine in hand, lips moving. Only when she was out of his sight had she allowed herself, briefly, to give way to tears at the prospect of the lonely weeks ahead without him. It had been several minutes before she had felt herself sufficiently in control to go back to the house.

She had looked in on Sophie. Nurse Griffin had been there before her, for the baby was tucked in as she had been before. Again she had been struggling and had half twisted over onto her stomach. Rachel had loosened the blankets and eased her onto her back.

That night she'd had the dream again. First the tapping at the window, then the face, rain pouring down it, mixing with the blood, dark holes where the eyes should have been. But this time it had not been a man's face. She had tried to see through the condensation on the inside of the windowpane, then she had wiped it away with her hand and seen that it was Sophie's face, etched by the black night, with blood running down her forehead. Sophie's face, red and puckered and screaming. She had heard the scream through the glass of the window, in spite of the noise of the storm.

She had wakened, terrified, but Bill had been beside her, had turned and taken her into his arms and soothed her, had helped her into Sophie's room, where she could see for herself that the baby was sleeping peacefully.

The next two days had been filled with his preparations for leaving, and she had made herself keep on the move so she would have less time to think about the empty weeks that stretched ahead.

She was still weakened by the shock and injuries of the crash, so at night she collapsed early into bed and slept heavily, gaining security from his presence. She found that she could push away memories of the accident and had become adept at forcing her thoughts into other channels—her increasing irritation with Nurse Griffin, for instance; redecoration of the house as soon as money became available; plans for keeping herself occupied while Bill was away. She would have time to write. She had not written anything since Sophie had been born, but the fiction editors of two magazines in the States, whom she had known well, had asked several times for stories. She might even earn enough to take Sophie to California to join Bill for a week or so toward the end of his stay. Her leg *must* be better by then.

When she told him this, he had put his arm around her shoulders and said, "Why not? Only I hope I'll be back in less time than it will take you to finish a story."

"It would be fun, though," she had said dreamily. "We could take a week off together, drive up the coast road and stay at San Simeon and Carmel."

"A second honeymoon?"

". . . and go on to the Napa Valley and Tahoe and maybe into Oregon. You've always said you wanted to go to Oregon."

"Not in winter."

"Somewhere else then. I'm going to work so hard I won't even have time to miss you."

The day before he left, she had offered to pack for him, but he preferred to do it himself, and their bedroom furniture was invisible under piles of clothes as he sorted and folded with brisk efficiency.

She had heard Sophie cry. When she opened the bedroom door Nurse Griffin was on her way along the corridor. "It's all right, I'll see to her," Rachel had said.

"You should rest your leg." There was an exasperating hint of reprimand.

"I was told to exercise it." She felt the angry glare of the hyperthyroid eyes on her back as she went into her child's room.

It was nearly five o'clock and the evening was clear, with a pale sun. She had decided to take the baby for a walk in her carriage, had wheeled her around the garden and onto the gravel path. Her leg was aching, but she tried not to limp. They went along the paddock fence at the back of the house and she thought again that the apple trees needed to come down. She would ask Charlie . . . she felt her mind try to wrench away, but she brought herself under control. Charlie was not here any longer to cut up firewood and do the other odd jobs. Charlie was dead. Charlie had been killed in her car.

At the end of the drive she saw something on the gate and remembered the welcome-home sign Bill had put up. It was time to take it down, and she thought she would put it away until *he* was due home.

But someone had added to it, scribbling two words in sprawling black writing so it now read, "Welcome home—you bitch!"

She looked at it for a moment in disbelief, then she tore it down and crumpled it. Who would do a thing like this? She shivered. It was *sick!* Was there someone out there who hated her enough to write those words? Why? For the first time, she felt a sense of dread. Bill was going away. She and Nurse Griffin would be alone in an isolated house, two women with a baby. Vulnerable. Then she thought, Stop it! It must have been one of the local kids, cruel, casual, unthinking. Not worth fussing about. She would not even tell Bill, it might worry him. But as she turned the carriage back toward the house she found herself searching the surroundings with frightened eyes. The sun had gone and a cold wind was blowing the first autumn leaves across the gravel. Was someone watching her even now? She walked more quickly and, for once, the looming bulk of the old house was a refuge.

She had not seen the dark animal shape that crouched, motionless, under the rhododendron bushes, absorbing all her movements.

Later that night, less than half a mile away, on the edge of the Lexton woods, the cat had gone hunting. Earlier it had stalked a rabbit that had come out from the edge of the forest and was feeding at the top end of the Chaters' paddock. It had been a long and exhausting stalk, for the rabbit had been nervous, sensing danger. The result was that it had fed in little bursts, moving quickly from place to place. Three times the cat had reached springing distance; three times the rabbit had hopped away. Finally, the cat had approached to within a few feet and lain behind the rotting stump of an old apple tree. This time the rabbit did not move. The cat crouched closer to the ground. Suddenly, like an uncoiling spring, its body shot forward. There was a moment of blinding pain in its rear paw. The pain came up into its throat in a half-expressed cry. It was enough for the rabbit. The sound gave it a split second's warning and it whisked away to one side and then raced for its burrow on the edge of the woods. The cat stood where the rabbit had been, its tail flicking angrily from side to side. It was starving. It had had nothing to eat all day.

With all senses alert, it came through the long grass of the paddock toward the dark house. Where the paddock gave way to lawn it paused, crouching in the shadow of a rhododendron bush; it watched and tested the air with its nose. It had lived in the wild now for nearly six years and the reason it had stayed alive was because it was cautious.

An owl hooted, but there was no other sound. Again, moving softly as a blown leaf, the cat approached the house. There was a smell of water and it was thirsty. It came to the lily pond and crouched, straining its neck until it was able to lap. Just then it saw a movement at one end of the pool. A young rabbit was being chased by a weasel. It raced along the grass and then, unable to stop, fell into the water. The weasel stopped, saw the cat, and disappeared into the night. The rabbit was moving in circles, trying to get out, but the overhang of the coping stones made this impossible. The cat watched its struggles and then, as it came to the edge for the second time, scooped it out with its paw and bit it at the base of the skull. The rabbit gave a single piercing scream. The cat carried it into the shadow of the rhododendron bush, where it ripped the warm body apart.

Rachel had heard the scream. This one was not in her dream, but real. What was out there? Rabbits screamed as they died. She had heard one before on a summer night and Bill had told her what it was. But that sound had been far away. This was close to the house.

In the time before he left, Bill had found someone to take Mrs. Aske's place, a girl named Penny Mason, who would come every day to clean and help with the baby. She was seventeen, a large plain young woman who moved and thought slowly. At first Rachel had wondered if Penny were mentally retarded; then she realized that she simply reacted at the gentle pace of the countryside.

Her eyes were wide apart and friendly and she had a nice, shy smile. One of their neighbors, Alec Webb, who knew her family, had recommended her.

"At least you'll have someone other than old Griffin for company during the day," Bill had said.

Penny had never done housework, except to help her mother, and Rachel had to show her everything and tell her everything. If she was not reminded to wipe the top of the coffee table, it wasn't wiped; if she wasn't told to vacuum under the furniture, it was not done; if she wasn't told to take a cloth and clean the whiskey and gin decanters, the dust was allowed to accumulate. She did not mind being told. A smile would lighten her round, vacant face and she would say, "Yes, Mrs. Chater. Sorry, Mrs. Chater. I'll do it now, Mrs. Chater."

She made up for any shortcomings by her attitude to Sophie. She doted on the baby and would happily have spent her entire day caring for her and playing with her, had Nurse Griffin allowed it. That was a plus as far as Rachel was concerned and, as Bill had said, she *was* company during the day.

"There's one snag," he had added. "She lives over at Addiscombe and has no transportation. You're going to have to fetch her in the morning and take her back in the evening. Which means driving. But with me away you'll have to drive anyway."

So they had gone into Chichester and bought Rachel a little Volkswagen with automatic transmission. She found, to her relief, that the fears of driving that had resulted from the accident evaporated as soon as she was behind the wheel and discovered that she could use her left foot on the brake. It took some getting used to; she kept on thinking that the brake was the clutch pedal, and the first two or three times she had to brake she nearly went through the windshield. But she quickly adapted to it and found that she could use her right foot for the accelerator with a minimum of pain.

3

The moment of Bill's departure had come all too soon. A taxi had arrived in the morning to take him to the airport. Up to the last moment, Rachel secretly wondered whether something might not be made to happen to stop him from going. If she fell down the stairs and damaged her knee again, would that be enough? If Sophie were to wake up with something wrong with her—nothing serious—would he cancel the flight? But as he had turned to kiss her on the front steps, she knew it was too late. She clung to him briefly, then forced herself to step back and smile.

"Look after yourself, darling. Don't talk to any strange women."

"I keep telling myself it's only six weeks," he said. "And there are telephones and letters. Write often, won't you?"

"Of course I will."

"You won't be nervous by yourself?"

"Good lord, no!" (*"Welcome home—you bitch!"*) "Anyhow, I'll have Nurse Griffin and Penny."

He kissed her again, hard, then ran to the taxi. Rachel, still in her dressing gown, had stood on the steps waving and watching until the car disappeared through the gates; then she had turned and gone inside.

A feeling of desolation and exhaustion had swept over her as she had seen, standing in the hall, the two women who would be virtually her only companions in the foreseeable future: Nurse Griffin, straight-backed and unsmiling, and Penny, covertly trying to attract Sophie's attention by waggling her fingers in front of her face and nodding her head so she looked half demented.

Rachel had slept badly. "I think I'm going back to bed for half an hour," she had said abruptly.

"I'll take Sophie," Nurse Griffin said.

"Oh, couldn't I put her to bed?" Penny had burst out. "Please, Mrs. Chater, just this once!"

The nurse glared at her and came forward. "I'll take her," she repeated.

It was an order, not a request. Deliberately, Rachel turned to Penny and handed her the child. "Of course you can. You've surely made a hit with her already, Penny."

Penny, unconscious of the tension, took Sophie upstairs, crooning to her. Nurse Griffin opened her mouth to say something, then closed it with a snap and turned on her heel.

As she wearily pulled herself up the stairs, Rachel wondered how long she was going to be able to endure Nurse Griffin. But without her she would be alone with Sophie in the house at night, and she did not like to think about that.

This time she had fallen asleep almost as soon as she had slipped under the sheets, and had not moved until the dream forced her back to life.

Now she made her way slowly downstairs. It was after midday and Penny was singing in the kitchen. There was no sign of Nurse Griffin and she felt a pang of guilt as she remembered their encounter earlier. After all, the woman had only been trying to do her job. It wasn't her fault that everything she did, every word she spoke, was an irritant. She's a natural disapprover, Rachel thought, but I guess she can't help being plain and charmless.

Once again she climbed the stairs, favoring her knee, and knocked at the nurse's bedroom door.

Nurse Griffin was standing by her bed. An open suitcase was lying on it.

"Look, why don't you and I spoil ourselves and have a sherry together before lunch?" Rachel said with exaggerated vivacity.

"No, thank you, Mrs. Chater. I don't drink." Her eyes looked huge behind the spectacles. "I have decided I shall be leaving today. Your leg is obviously on the mend and you have that girl to help you now." There was venom in the way she said "that girl."

"But Sophie . . ."

"I cannot believe one woman and a baby need *two* people to attend to them. I should be grateful if you would drop me at the station in Addiscombe when you take the girl home."

I'm not going to beg her, Rachel thought. "If that's what you want," she said with formal politeness, "I'm very pleased you were able to come at all."

So she was to be on her own in this rambling house with its dark, secret corners after all.

Without much hope, she went into the kitchen. "Penny, Nurse Griffin is leaving. I suppose you couldn't live in for a while, could you? Just until my husband gets back."

There was a long silence as the wheels of Penny's mind creaked into motion, then she shook her head. "I couldn't, Mrs. Chater," she said. "It's my mum. She hasn't been well and I'm the oldest, see. She can manage during the day, but there are five of us and I've got to be home to put the small ones to bed."

"It was just a thought," Rachel said wistfully.

At that moment the telephone rang in Bill's study. She limped in to answer it.

"Rachel? It's Moira Renshaw. My dear, how *are* you? Bill told us you were due home from hospital."

"Much better, thank you."

"I can't tell you how bad I feel . . . not coming to see you . . . but the days pass so quickly." She was talking fast to cover her embarrassment. "Anyhow, you're back. Super for Bill, and, why I'm ringing, could you both come and have a drink with us this evening? We suddenly thought . . . could you?"

"I'm afraid Bill has just left for America."

"Oh." There was a pause and a noticeable diminution of enthusiasm. "Wouldn't you come anyway?"

"I don't . . ." she began, then thought of the day and evening stretching ahead. "I'd love to."

"That's marvelous, if you're sure you feel up to it. Are you driving yet?"

"Yes."

"Super. There'll only be Alec Webb and Celia James."

"Celia James? I don't think I know her."

"She's just moved into the thatched cottage near us. I think you'll like her. She's going to collect Alec in her car."

As she hung up the telephone Rachel thought wryly that she must be desperate to be so pleased at an invitation from the Renshaws, whom she did not much like. David Renshaw was the biggest landowner in the area, a large, ponderous man in his middle fifties, very conscious of his money and standing. He seemed to have taken to Bill and felt they had at least one bond, because he had once farmed cattle in Central Africa and Bill had lived for a time in Nairobi, where his widowed mother had been housekeeper in a large hotel. She had heard David refer to them both, with heavy humor, as "old Africa hands." Moira was younger than her husband, a fluffy, rather silly woman who hunted celebrities relentlessly. She had been delighted to discover that her new neighbor, William Chater, was a novelist of some note. Rachel had always felt that Moira endured her only as an appendage to Bill.

They were all gathered in the Renshaws' drawing room when she arrived, clutching Sophie's portable crib.

There was a flurry of welcome and David Renshaw bore Sophie off to the nearest bedroom.

When he returned he beamed at her. He was a big man, overweight and with a high color. "The beauteous Mrs. Chater," he said with heavy gallantry. "No wheelchair?"

She felt the surge of irritation which, she now remembered, she always felt in his company. "That's very perceptive of you," she said coldly.

There was a moment of embarrassed silence, then Moira said hastily, "It's so nice to have you back."

"And what's the news of the great author?" Renshaw said. "Still writing?"

It was another in that series of routine questions put by people uneasy in the presence of those who, they clearly considered, worked at abnormal occupations. David said the same thing every time they met. "Yes, still writing," she said. "And you? Still farming?"

He was taken aback for a moment and then he said, "Of course. Why do you ask?"

"Just checking up. Hello, Alec."

Alec Webb came forward to kiss her with real affection. He was the only person apart from Bill who had taken the trouble to visit her in the hospital.

They had met when he had called on them a few days after Rachel's arrival from America. He had been a member of the Long Range Desert Group during the war in North Africa—some sort of quasi-private army, as Rachel understood it, whose function had been to operate behind the German lines—and his armored car had taken a direct hit. The left side of his face had been badly burnt. They had brought him back to East Grinstead and the surgeon Archibald McIndoe had worked on his face, taking pieces of skin from the inside of his thigh and grafting them onto his left cheek and the left side of his forehead. But the skin was lighter than the rest of his face and gave him a patchwork look. He had lost his left eye and wore a glass one, and now his right eye, having taken the strain for so many years, was beginning to fail. Once Rachel, calling on him unexpectedly, had seen him through a window, blindfolded and moving around his sitting room as though playing a macabre game of blind man's buff by himself. It had taken her a few seconds to realize that he was practicing for the day when he could no longer see at all. Over the months she had come to respect and admire his determination not to give in to his disability.

He was a widower and lived about half a mile from the Chaters in a cottage in the woods. After the war he had become a veterinary surgeon and had run a rural practice in Addiscombe, Lexton's nearest small town. Because of his failing eyesight he had retired early. His wife Mary had died soon afterwards.

After their first meeting, Bill and Rachel had become his friends. Rachel went to see him often and, since he could no longer drive a car, had taken him for drives over the Downs or to the sea at West Wittering. He would join them for a meal at least once a week. He never whined, never spoke about the future, and filled his days listening to the radio and making his own wine.

"Sit down, love," he said now. "That leg can't be right yet."

She smiled at him gratefully and allowed herself to be led to a chair as Moira Renshaw brought another woman forward.

"This is Celia James," Moira said. "A new neighbor, Rachel, as I told you."

She was a tall woman wearing a gray woolen dress that clung to her. Although she was slender her breasts were heavy and her hips curved down in ripe lines from a narrow waist. Her thin, aquiline face was striking, with hollow cheeks under a smooth cap of black hair. She made Rachel feel suddenly shabby and unkempt, but her smile was friendly.

"Hullo!" she said. "Alec told me about your accident, but it seems superfluous to ask how you are. You look wonderful. Hospital must have been good for you."

Rachel said, "I guess everyone should go in once a year, if only to make them appreciate their own homes. It's like knocking your head on the wall: so nice when you stop."

There was a pause as they digested the aphorism, testing it, until Renshaw laughed loudly: "I like that!"

Alec brought her a drink, then moved to stand beside Celia. Rachel glanced from one to the other and her eyes widened at his expression. He was looking at Celia like a schoolboy in love for the first time.

Celia turned to her. "I do hope your husband's coming," she said. "I've read all his books and I'm longing to meet him."

"Oh, dear, I forgot to tell you," Moira said. "Bill's in America, isn't he, Rachel?"

"He left this morning."

"A bit sudden, wasn't it?" Alec said.

"He only had three days notice. He has to work on a screenplay in Hollywood."

"How long will he be away?" Celia said.

"He hopes not more than six weeks or so."

"So you're by yourself?"

"I have a daily help, and there's my daughter for company."

"I heard you'd had a baby recently. What's her name?"

"Sophie."

"David, Celia's glass is empty," Moira said. Celia smiled at Renshaw as she handed him her glass. She was undoubtedly an attractive woman, and Rachel found herself not too sorry that Bill was not present. She had looked at herself in the mirror before she left home and not liked what she'd seen. Her face seemed gaunt and dead, there were new lines under her blue eyes, and her hair, though washed the previous day, hung lankly to her shoulders. Normally a rich autumn brown, it looked dry and lifeless. She felt years older than she had before the accident and was sure she looked it. There had been disappointment in Celia's face when she had heard Bill was away, and Rachel, at this moment, felt herself incapable of competing with women who found her husband attractive, not only for his appearance but for the successful novels that had brought him some fame, if an erratic income.

She sat, half listening as the conversation swirled above her.

She had only arrived in Lexton shortly before Sophie had been born, when Bill was too immersed in his last book to be bothered with socializing. When he was working he preferred to cut himself off from distractions. She had not minded, because she had not been well and, when she felt strong enough, was busy organizing her new home. Then the child had arrived and she had suffered an unpleasant bout of postnatal depression when everything was too much effort, when her imagination, vivid at the best of times, ran riotously over the field of life's horrors: Bill was tiring of her; something would happen to take Sophie from her; nameless pains that plagued her at night were cancer, heart trouble, arthritis. On the whole, she managed to keep the depression to herself, apart from the occasional bout of weeping that Bill had attributed to general debility after childbirth, but it had been a strain and she had avoided contact with strangers. Almost the only outsider she had seen was Alec, whose company was never a strain. Then, miraculously, she had awakened one morning to a glorious day and the clouds over her mind had disappeared. Her natural optimism had surfaced and life, on the whole, looked good. She had decided to face the world again and had started by contacting the Renshaws, whom she had met casually once or twice, and asking them for drinks. She recognized that she and Bill had little in common with them, but in time they might be the means of widening her circle of acquaintances.

But not long after her emergence there had been the accident, and once more she had been removed from circulation. Now, watching the party, which seemed flat to her without Bill, she wondered whether she could, in fact, bear much more of the Renshaws.

David turned to Alec. ". . . To go on with what I was saying before Rachel arrived, if the Reds get a foothold in Southern Africa, we've had it. Take my word for it, they'll control the sea route around the Cape and have their subs and missile carriers deep into the Indian Ocean and the South Atlantic . . ."

Alec nodded abstractedly, his eyes on Celia.

Suddenly aware that Rachel was being left out of the conversation, Moira turned and said, "The last time we saw you, Bill was talking about having a wood stove installed to save oil. Is it working yet?"

"Yes. It's very successful."

"It must have cost something," Renshaw said.

"Bill says it will pay for itself within a year."

"That's all very well, but it presupposes an unlimited supply of wood . . ."

Rachel had noticed Alec glance at her and knew why. Now he broke in: "When I was in North Africa we booby-trapped a wood stove once . . ."

She smiled to herself. "When I was in North Africa . . ." was one of Alec's catch-phrases. He was dwelling more and more in the past and sometimes she grew weary of his wartime reminiscences. But she told herself that the past was all he had, since the future was unimaginable. Unless Celia . . . but it was too early even to hope that Alec would have such luck.

". . . Not a big chap like yours. A small French one. We taped the gelignite inside the firebox. Rather hoped we might get Rommel. It was one of those times when the Germans and us were going backwards and forwards over a single piece of the desert like a tennis ball. Anyway, it went off with a hell of a bang. When we went to look, all we found were three dead Arabs, no Jerries at all. Arabs must have come in to shelter and lit the fire . . . and up she went. I remember another booby trap in Libya . . ."

Moira, who thought almost as slowly as Penny at times, was

not listening to him. "Oh, my God, Rachel," she broke in. "How awful of me even to have mentioned it! I'd completely forgotten. That was the stove Charlie Leech was putting in the night—"

"The night I had the accident," Rachel said.

"Yes, well, oh, God! I'm making it worse. How *is* the leg?"

"Not too bad. It will always be a little stiff."

"Isn't it lucky . . . I mean . . ."

"Yes," Rachel said sharply. "Isn't it?"

"Well . . ." Moira was seeking frantically for a change of subject. "Well—aren't we lucky to have attracted Celia to our little village? *So* nice to see a new face."

"Especially such a pretty one," said her husband, predictably.

"What brought you here?" Rachel said. "Did you know anyone in the area?"

"Not a soul," Celia said cheerfully. "I'd been living up north and I wanted a change. The weather's so foul in Yorkshire and I've always preferred the south, anyway. I spent a few weeks driving around Hampshire and Sussex and I saw a dozen or more houses before I found the one I bought. I love it."

"What took you to Yorkshire in the first place?" Alec said. "You don't look like a North C-oontry lass."

She laughed at his broad accent. "What *do* I look like?"

Again Rachel noticed the unusual softness in his face as he spoke to Celia. "The owner of a penthouse in Mayfair, maybe."

"Belgravia. Eaton Square." Moira chimed in.

"The Bishop's Avenue, Hampstead," David said, but by now the laughter was becoming forced.

I'm going to have to get used to it, she told herself as she drove home, slowly and carefully, her left foot poised above the brake pedal. They tell me how lucky I am, and then there's a pause and we all think about Charlie, who was not lucky. They don't mean to be crass. It's just a way of making conversation.

She reached the house, put the car away and limped inside, carrying Sophie, who had slept throughout the evening. After tucking her up, Rachel went into the sitting room and stared at the big, black Norwegian stove, remembering Charlie, muscles rippling, chest bare, heaving it into place.

Sometime she would have to face what had happened, think it through, remember it. Didn't psychiatrists make their patients dig down into their subconscious and face thoughts they were trying to avoid?

But not now. Not yet. She forced her mind away from Charlie, to Bill. Where was he at this moment? What would he be doing tomorrow? Working? Or playing? He would not be with Talini all the time. Who else would he see? She wondered if he had ever had affairs when he had been in Los Angeles before. She remembered the kids she had known who were trying to make it in the movies and television. They would sleep with anyone to get a part, no matter how small. Even the waitresses and the secretaries were good-looking and on the make.

Stop it!

She poured herself a stiff whiskey. At least tonight she had forgotten the cat for a while. But perhaps it had been there, lying in the bushes beside the road, watching as she had driven past. She shivered, finished her drink and went up to bed. But again she found difficulty in sleeping; her mind went always to the cat, the black cat . . .

First the tapping . . . then the face . . .

But this time it was not a human face. She was unable to see it clearly but she knew it was not human. She began to move toward the window. Floating in slow motion, walking on air, a foot or two above the floor, ghostlike . . .

She saw a hairy face with green, staring eyes and a head so dark it merged with the night. Then the sharp teeth . . . the pink tongue . . .

Drawn as though on a string, unable to resist, she saw her hand go out and wipe away the condensation on the windowpane. It was there. The cat's face. With blood on its head . . .

The next morning, with memories of the sweating fear that had woken her, she decided to buy a dog. Neither she nor Bill had ever owned one, but now a dog would not only be company, but a guard.

Her resolve was hardened when she went to the back door and saw that some animal had knocked the lid off one of the big garbage cans during the night and that there was rubbish scattered over the yard. Had she heard the noise through her heavy sleep? Had the crash of the lid been part of her dream? She could not remember, but the thought that she had slept through it frightened her. She was alone in the house with Sophie. What would happen if something was wrong with the baby and she did not hear her cry out?

As soon as she had fetched Penny from Addiscombe, she drove to Alec's cottage. He came out to greet her.

"This is a nice surprise. Come and have some coffee."

"Later, if I may. Alec, I want a dog."

"Good idea," he said. "Should have suggested it to you before."

"Where do I get one?"

"There are some boarding kennels up past the Renshaws. Run by the Pets' Defence League. You should find one there."

"What's the Pets' Defence League?"

"They keep strays for a time and if no one claims them, they're destroyed. Unless they get the offer of a good home. Want me to come with you?"

"I'd like that."

"Of course it's a lottery," he said in the car. "You can never tell what sort of character a dog might have. You could get a bad animal, but on the other hand, I've heard of marvelous successes people have had with strays."

Richmond Kennels comprised a series of concrete and wire cages in two parallel lines behind a square, red-tiled bungalow. The place had an air of neglect and seediness.

A young man came out of the bungalow. He was dressed in an anorak and rubber boots and his hair was down to his shoulders.

"We're looking for a dog that will make a good pet as well as a watchdog," Alec said.

"I dunno . . ." He rubbed the side of his face with a hand that was ingrained with dirt. "There aren't many."

Most of the dogs seemed to be small terriers or crossbreeds. There was a strong smell of damp coats, urine, and disinfectant. The dogs jumped up against the wire, barking.

"What about that one?" Rachel said, pointing to a black and white border collie.

Alec shook his head. "That's a working sheep dog. They need things to do. You want something like a . . . what about that one over there? The golden Labrador?"

The dog stood in the middle of its run, growling.

The young man let Alec into the cage and it backed away, still growling, to its straw bed in the concrete shelter.

"Good boy," Alec said softly. "Good boy. Come on." He went forward, holding his hand out, not making any sudden movement. The dog bared its teeth and began to bark. "Good boy. Come on, now."

He waited patiently, gradually moving closer. His soft voice acted hypnotically and after a while the barking gave way to a growl and even that ceased and the dog allowed his hand to touch it. He stroked it and kept the tone of his voice even as he said, "What happened to him?"

"They brought him in the van. He was found down by Harting, tied to a tree. Wire around his neck. Been like that for two days, they said."

Alec raised the muzzle to look at the teeth. His hands ran along the body and down the forepaws and under the stomach. "He seems all right. He probably only needs kindness."

"I'll take him," Rachel said.

On the way home they bought a basket and Alec spent a happy, busy half-hour constructing a run from some chicken wire near the back door to hold the dog until he was used to his new territory.

"What are you going to call him?" he asked as they sat later in the kitchen having a cup of coffee.

"Franco," she said. "After Talini, who's going to make our fortune for us. Alec, Celia James seems nice. What do you think?"

He shot her a glance and she saw a flush start red patches on his scarred face.

"She is," he said.

"How long have you known her?"

"She only moved here a few weeks ago. I met her at the Renshaws'. We've had dinner together once or twice. She's an interesting and intelligent woman. Attractive, too, don't you think?"

"Very."

"Rachel, am I just a bloody fool?" he said suddenly. "It's the first time since Mary died that any woman . . . She doesn't seem to notice this, either." He touched his ruined face.

"Of course she doesn't! *Nobody* does, Alec. I wonder what made her settle in Lexton?"

"She said she liked Sussex. I thought she might be lonely, but she said no, she was used to living by herself."

"Has she ever been married?"

"Oh, yes. She's Mrs. James. A widow, I believe." He stood up. "I must go. Celia has asked me in for a drink before lunch. She's looking forward to seeing you again."

When he had stumped off she went out to Franco's run and tried to make friends with him. At first she had little success. He seemed uneasy in her presence. Then she took him inside to the little passage that led to the kitchen, and showed him his basket, which she had padded with an old blanket. He stepped into it, scrabbled around for a moment, then sat down. He still jerked his head away when she tried to pat him until finally she fetched a packet of dog biscuits and began feeding him. "I'll *buy* your damn affection!" she said. "Here." He sniffed the piece of biscuit, then took it. When she did not immediately offer another, he pushed his nose into her hand and peered anxiously up into her face. As she handed him the biscuit and patted his soft, golden fur she felt a dawning fondness for him. "We'll get along," she said, and was irrationally delighted when, for the first time, his tail twitched.

Suddenly, he looked past her, through the open door toward the garden. He stood up and the hairs on his back rose as he began to bark. Rachel moved back, wondering what had upset him. He jumped from the box and streaked out, past his run, toward the rhododendron bushes near the drive. She followed and found him nosing in the bushes. As she bent toward him to grab his collar, she heard a rustle and a black shape streaked from the far side of the bushes, across the paddock, and disappeared into the undergrowth.

"Franco! Get it!" she shouted. "Cat, Franco!"

But he was no longer interested, because he had found something else under the bush: pieces of furry skin, some bones smeared with blood. As he worried at them, Rachel felt queasy. She remembered the scream she had heard in the night.

The cat was a female and had no name. No one had ever called it anything other than "the cat" or "that cat" or "that bloody cat." It had lived an existence of almost total isolation except on two occasions when it had mated with toms belonging to nearby farms. The first time was when it was three years old. It had had a litter of four kittens. A fox had taken two, a third had wandered away from the den and been attacked and eaten by crows. It had brought the fourth to maturity but it had long since left the area to seek its own territory. The cat had mated again a year ago but the kittens had been born dead and it had taken each of the small limp bodies in its mouth and put them beneath an elder bush about two hundred yards from the den.

When the dog drove it from the shelter of the bush it ran across the lawn and into the deep grass of the paddock. There were paths leading to the forest, but like all feral cats it kept clear of them, forcing its own passage through the tangled undergrowth until it came to its den.

This had once been a badger set and was hidden among a tangled mass of beech roots and wild willow, invisible to the naked eye. The cat went through the screen of willow, entered the den and curled up to sleep. But sleep did not come easily. It was hungry, for in twenty-four hours all it had eaten was part of a squirrel that had been killed by a car. But it was not only hunger that kept it awake. The bones in its left back paw were not knitting. One splinter had pierced the skin and an infection had set in around it. It began to lick the paw, trying to soothe the ache with its warm rough tongue. It spent much of the day dozing and much of it licking the paw and when the afternoon began to fade it came out of the den and lay in the screen of willow looking down toward the house. It had left the rhododendron bush not because of the dog's presence—it was not afraid of dogs—but because of Rachel. It was afraid of human beings. But hunger was inexorable and as dusk crept across the fringe of the Great Forest and mist began to form in the hidden valleys of the Downs, it left the cover and moved down again to the edge of the paddock where it could watch the house, the source of food.

4

Rachel arrived home from taking Penny to Addiscombe a few minutes after six o'clock. After the warm day the earth was rapidly losing its heat and skeins of mist were forming around the house. She opened the back of the little car and reached in for Sophie's portable crib. As she pulled it out, she froze. She had a feeling that someone was near, that she was being watched. She glanced over her shoulder. She could see no one; there was no sound but the rustling of leaves as the breeze stirred the bushes. She told herself it was her imagination, but that didn't help and she hurried inside, closing and locking the front door behind her.

She had rested most of the afternoon while Penny had entertained the baby and her knee was feeling better. She had done her exercises and they, too, seemed to have helped. But now it began to throb again with the crib's weight. She took Sophie upstairs and bathed her. Afterwards the baby went to sleep without complaint, somewhat to Rachel's regret. She would have liked Sophie's company.

It was almost dark and she brought Franco in and gave him some biscuits in a little milk. "I'm going to light the fire. Why don't you come and lie in front of it like a proper dog?" she said. But when he had finished the food he made for his basket in the passage. She locked the back door and put up the chain. She checked that the front door was still locked and bolted, and closed the drawing-room curtains, pulling the house around her. She started a fire in the cast-iron stove and soon the wood was blazing. Then she stood in the middle of the drawing room and thought, This is the worst time, and it's going to be the worst

time every day. Don't let it get to you. Don't think about it. Do
something. Anything. Knit, sew, read, watch television. Just do
something.

Normally, it was the best time of the day. Bill would come in
after his bath and pour drinks and they would be comfortable
together and watch television or listen to music or read, not feeling they had to talk, just being together. Will I have a whiskey,
she thought? Yes, I will. She sat in front of the TV with her
glass, wishing she knew someone well enough to call and invite
them to join her. Even the Renshaws—but she had just been
there, and she could not bother Alec again.

For the first time a feeling of self-pity threatened to sweep
over her. Whoa, she thought, there are millions of people like
you and millions worse off. Get a grip on yourself. But there was
another voice inside her that said, You're alone. No one here
gives a damn about you.

And then the doorbell rang.

It was like a scream in the night and for a second her heart
stopped. She rose, confused and unsure of what to do. It rang
again. From the depths of the house the dog began to bark. She
went into the hall and switched on the outside light. The front
door had bolts but no chain and she wished there was a fisheye
peephole that would show her who was outside. She wanted to
shout, "Who is it?" but felt she would sound foolish. She drew
the bolt and opened the door. Celia James was standing on the
steps, wearing a long, moss-green loden coat and a white scarf at
her throat.

"Hi!" Rachel said. "Come on in."

"I knew you were by yourself and I thought you might be
feeling like some company," Celia said.

"You were right. I was wishing someone would drop by. Let
me get you a drink."

Celia asked for Scotch and water, then said, "How are you
getting on by yourself? I've lived alone for so long I'm used to it,
but I remember how awful it was at first when—when my husband wasn't there."

"I manage pretty well," Rachel said. "I'm so lucky that Bill
will be back."

Celia's vivid face was shadowed for a moment, then she

looked up and smiled. "Tell me about yourself, Rachel. I've read your husband's books and Alec tells me you're a writer, too."

"I used to do short stories and television scripts."

"I envy you. I've always wanted to do something creative."

"I haven't written a line since Sophie was born."

"But you could if you wanted to. It's there, inside you, the ability, the knowledge that at any time you could take a piece of paper and create people and events. You don't know how lucky you are."

"Have you tried?"

"Often, but I can't put my thoughts down accurately or consecutively."

"It's practice, like everything else."

"How did you start?"

"I used to write when I was in college. My father was a newspaperman. Writing was the only thing I knew. I never considered doing anything else. Let me give you another drink."

Rachel sipped her second whiskey and felt the tension begin to melt out of her muscles and a slight buzz in her head.

"What did you do when you left college?"

"I was lucky. *Time* magazine took me on as a researcher."

"And then?"

"That lasted a couple of years. I was selling short stories at the same time. It was more my scene than newsgathering or checking facts, so when I was offered the chance to become assistant fiction-editor of one of the women's glossies I jumped at it. I stayed in New York for another four or five years writing and editing and doing the occasional TV script. Then Paramount offered me a job as a story editor and I went back to the West Coast."

She paused. "I'm talking too much. Tell me about your cottage. Have you had much redecorating to do?"

"A great deal, but I've enjoyed it. You must come and see it. At the moment it's a mess, and work seems to have come to a halt. But I love it here, don't you? The people are all so friendly, I find. You and your husband must have loads of friends already."

"No, we haven't. We've been sort of closed in since I arrived from the States. First Sophie was born and it took me a while to recover, then—then there was the accident."

Celia shook her head sympathetically. "That must have been dreadful. I knew Charlie Leech."

"Really?" Rachel did not want to discuss Charlie.

"He'd been recommended as a marvelous workman, so I hired him. He had been at the cottage, on and off, for about ten days, painting and decorating."

Rachel said nothing. So that was why he had not come to install the stove on the day arranged. She remembered how angry Bill had been when he had not turned up. If he *had* come then, Bill would have been home and it would never have happened . . .

The other woman seemed to sense her unease and changed the subject. "How did you meet your husband? Was it here or in America?"

"In California. I was living there."

Celia waited for her to continue, but Rachel felt suddenly reluctant to discuss herself and Bill with a stranger, no matter how charming and sympathetic she was.

"I'm asking too many questions," Celia said quickly. "It's a bad habit, but I'm interested in people and I've enjoyed your husband's books."

"Don't apologize. It's nice to know he has one reader at least! He's halfway through a new book now."

"I'm always fascinated by how writers work. Does he keep office hours or write when the inspiration strikes?"

There it was again, the implication that an author awaited some mysterious force to move him to work.

"He works more or less office hours in his room at the bottom of the garden," Rachel said. "But he also spends hours sitting and thinking, out in the sun or in front of the fire. Sometimes he works out the entire plot of a book when it would look to an outsider as though he's simply wasting time."

"And then he puts it down on a typewriter, or by hand?"

"He's taken to using a little tape recorder, then he has it typed by an agency. He's already filled several cassettes, though the book isn't half finished. There's a stack of them in his room. He's taken the manuscript with him and he hopes he might have time to work on it between sessions on the screenplay."

"What a lovely life it sounds. Do you enjoy having him home all the time?"

"I love it. In the States women whose husbands have retired tend to moan that they married them for better or worse—but not for lunch. I've never been able to understand that."

Celia laughed and stood up. "Time to go. We must do this more often, now we're both bachelor girls."

"Call in whenever you can." As they reached the door Rachel added: "The mist is coming down. You'll have to drive carefully."

"I nearly hit a cat on the way here."

"Which one?"

"Which one? God knows. There are so many. I thought it might be yours, but you don't own one, do you?"

"No, why?"

"It was sitting in your drive when I turned in. Then it ran off. Seemed to be limping."

"Was it big? I mean, bigger than usual?"

"Yes."

"That goddamned cat is haunting me," Rachel burst out, an emotional chill mixing with her anger. "It's been raiding the garbage can and I think it killed and ate something on the lawn."

"I'd poison it if I were you." It was said coolly, a piece of practical country advice. "Strychnine's the best. I used it on a stray dog once."

"I bought a dog today. He sleeps inside but I hope his presence might drive the cat away. It gives me the creeps. I have a feeling it watches me."

Celia laughed. "I think you're overreacting."

After she had gone, Rachel went upstairs to look at Sophie. The baby had flung off her thermal blanket and was lying in a twisted mass of arms and legs. "Penny says I should tuck you up tightly, too," Rachel whispered. "Maybe she and Nurse Griffin are right."

That day the baby had cried after lunch and not even a cracker would calm her. It was only after Penny had taken her in her arms for a few moments, then put her in the crib and tucked the blankets up to her chin and deep down on either side of the mattress that she had finally gone to sleep. "Why do you tuck her in so tightly?" Rachel had asked. Penny had looked confused, her big, moonlike face turning toward Rachel like a radar dish. "Can't say," she replied. And then, as her brain slowly sorted out the correct response, she had added, "Mum always makes it like that. She says it makes them feel more secure, like."

Now Sophie lay like a little Russian doll and Rachel realized that she herself liked the blankets tucked around her. Bill slept any which way, flinging his arms and legs out, but she was a neat sleeper. Maybe Sophie had inherited a need for such security from her.

She glanced at her watch. It was nine-thirty. What now? Bed? Her mind protested. It was too early for bed. But the well-being engendered by Celia's visit and two whiskeys was wearing off. She returned to the sitting room and switched on the television, but hardly watched it. She had imagined that the beginning of the evening would be the worst time. What about later? What about when she switched off the light, when she only had her own thoughts to live with and the dream was waiting in the dark corridors of sleep. Would another drink help, or would it make her more wide-awake? She wouldn't know unless she had one. Good old Scotch, she thought. A drink for all seasons. She poured one, put her leg up on the footstool, and sat back, trying to concentrate on the television screen. The whiskey and the warmth of the fire soon made her sleepy and she dozed.

She awoke a little after midnight. The last program being over, the test card was on the television screen; the fire had burned low, and she was cold. This time there was no dream but her heart was beating at twice its normal speed, as though something had given her a fright; not an image, but a noise.

She strained to listen. She thought she heard a high-pitched note, almost like the creaking of a rusty door. Then a scraping noise of metal on stone. It came from the rear of the house. Then a thud. And again the scraping.

She was tempted to go to Sophie's room and lock herself in with the child, symbolically burying her head under the blankets and waiting for whatever was causing the noise to go away. But she knew that the childlike course was closed to her by the years of adulthood. She picked up a brass fire-iron and went into the hall. The high-pitched noise was clearer; then she heard a scratching. It sounded as though an animal were trying to get into the house. Where is that goddamned dog, she thought? This is why I bought him.

"Franco!" she said loudly. "What is it, boy?"

The high-pitched noise changed timbre and she realized what it was: it was the dog, whining. She went into the kitchen, switched on all the lights and opened the door into the back passage. Franco was at the far end, at the back door, scratching to get out.

"What is it, Franco?"

The sound of her voice caused him to bark and jump up at the door. She switched on the light in the yard. The back door had two small glass windows near the top and by standing on tiptoe she could see out. One of the garbage cans was on its side and a mess was strewn over the concrete. The lid had fallen and rolled. She thought she saw a black shape move in the penumbra of the light but could not be sure.

Her fear gave way to anger. The dog was barking hysterically, jumping up and trying to get out. "All right," she said, "you want to get that cat, you get it." She opened the door. Franco shot out like a golden streak and she followed him, set the can upright, and put a couple of bricks on the lid. Then she banged the door, locked and chained it, and stood with her back to it.

She was wide-awake. She kept on all the lights and made herself a cup of coffee, took it back into the sitting room, built up the fire, and put a record on the stereo. She lit a cigarette and sat down. But she was restless. She stood up and began to pace slowly up and down the room. Her leg ached, but in a curious way she was glad of the pain; it gave her something to think about.

First the tapping . . .

She stopped, holding her breath.

She could have sworn she heard tapping. But it was supposed to come in her dream, not in reality. Her back was to the window and she was afraid to turn. What would she see? But the curtains were drawn. Slowly, by force of will, she made herself turn around. There was nothing. But she had the sensation of the house around her turning and twisting in a life of its own.

Where *was* the tapping? In her head? The fear of fear itself swept over her. She went to the back of the house, opened the door on the chain and called, "Franco! Franco!" She called for five minutes, but there was no sign of the dog.

She found herself back in the sitting room, not knowing how she had got there. She lit a cigarette and crossed to the drinks table and picked up her glass. She was about to pour herself another whiskey when she realized that she was in a moment of crisis in her life and that there was no one to help her resolve it except herself. She put the decanter down.

"All right, face it," she said aloud.

Her father had often told her that when you actually faced a problem it never seemed as bad as it had before.

"So do it!" She seemed to hear his voice.

She knew what she had to face. She had to remember the night of the accident, to dig each detail out of her memory and look at it, and then, if her father was right, the fear would have disappeared.

5

Bill had gone up to London to have dinner and spend the night with his editor. It was a hot, sultry day and the clouds had built up after lunch into great purple thunderheads. The atmosphere was electric and very close. She had taken Sophie and Alec Webb into Chichester, shopping, and had returned home at five o'clock. She was preparing Sophie's supper when there was a knock at the back door. Charlie Leech was standing in the yard.

"I've got the elbow pipe for your stove," he said, holding out a piece of seven-inch black vitreous enamel piping with a right-angle bend.

"Are you going to do it now? Mr. Chater's in London. He was expecting you last Monday."

"Couldn't make it then. It won't take long."

She led him through into the sitting room, where the black stove stood on its three legs in the fireplace. Bill had had the small Edwardian coal-burning fire removed and they had found a large, square inglenook fireplace behind it. Then he had bought the big Jøtul and asked Charlie, the village handyman, to install it.

She knew Bill always gave him a glass of beer when he arrived to do a job and she asked if he would like one now.

"I don't mind," he said, which was his way of showing enthusiasm.

She took a can from the refrigerator and gave it to him. He ripped off the tag and put the can to his lips.

She was never sure of Charlie. Bill had an easy way of dealing with workmen. He was friendly and made jokes with them and

called them by their Christian names and they were friendly and
joked with him, but they called him sir or Mr. Chater. It was the
same with Charlie. But she called him Mr. Leech because she
had the distinct feeling that if she called him Charlie he might—
though not in Bill's presence—decide he had the right to call her
Rachel.

He was in his mid-thirties and had the reputation of being the
village stud. His thick black hair was combed back in a duck's
tail, reminding her of pictures she had seen of the 1950s teddy
boys. He had a broad, heavy face and wore a single gold ring in
his right ear. It was apparent that he was vain of his appearance,
and he would take off his shirt when he was working, even on
cool days. Now it was unbuttoned to his navel, showing a substantial bronzed chest. On the inner part of his left forearm was
a tattoo of an anchor, and he liked to give an impression that he
had spent part of his life at sea and been around the world a
couple of times. In reality, the farthest he had ever been from
home, apart from jaunts to London, was a day trip to Boulogne
on the French Channel coast, where he had drunk red wine and
brandy and been sick as a dog on the ship coming home.

There were stories about him: that he was a poacher, that he'd
had affairs with most of the married women in the district, that
he was the father of half a dozen illegitimate children, that he
came from Gypsy stock.

He finished the beer in one long swallow and wiped his mouth
with the back of his hand. "Coming on to storm," he remarked,
peering at the empty can.

"Would you like another?" she said.

"I don't mind." He added with a wink, "Not trying to get me
drunk, are you?"

She took the can from him and their fingers touched and she
read a knowing look in his dark brown eyes. It seemed to say,
"You and me are equals, aren't we?" She knew the look would
never appear when Bill was around, for without effort he pre-
served the dividing line between employer and employee, but
she sensed that Charlie considered Americans to be free and
easy and equal, all working-class people together.

She handed him another can and said coolly, "I have things to
do."

She went upstairs and bathed Sophie. She took her time because she could hear him working and she wanted to see as little of him as possible. Finally she came down with Sophie in her arms. He was hammering at something in the fireplace and only his feet were visible.

"Are you having problems?" she said.

He emerged. He was naked from the waist up, a powerfully built man covered in a sheen of sweat on which brick dust stood out in tiny pink spots.

"I've got to cut them bricks," he said. "Otherwise the flue won't go up the chimney. It's too tight."

She fed Sophie in the kitchen, put the plates in the dishwasher, and tidied up. He was still hammering. She took the baby upstairs, played with her, then put her down to sleep.

Thunder rolled over the Downs. She stood at Sophie's window for a while, watching the lightning crackle through the darkening sky. She waited until the child was asleep and then she listened for hammering from downstairs. It had stopped.

When she went down Charlie was moving the huge black stove further into the inglenook. Bill had told her that it weighed more than four hundred pounds. She stood in the doorway. The muscles in Charlie's back were standing out like cables. He was grunting and heaving, and slowly the stove moved back, the flue pipe bedding down into the hole he had cut in the bricks. He gave a last grunt and stood back to look at his work. He was breathing heavily and she saw that his hair was matted and caked with dust.

"Bloody thing!" he said.

"But you've got it in."

"As the actress said to the bishop. It's not level. Look . . ." He pointed to the front legs, which were slightly off the hearth. "Can't leave it like that." He rummaged in his tool bag and came up with two washers. "I'll lift. You put one under each leg." She knelt on the hearth. Her head was close to his body and her face was within inches of his stomach. He heaved and the stove came up.

"Quickly!"

She slipped a washer under one foot.

"Now for the other," he said. "Ready?"

The smell of his body was in her nostrils, an overpoweringly musty odor of sweat.

"I'm ready."

"Right. One. Two. Three."

She could almost hear his muscles groan under the strain. The stove came up and she slipped the washer under the second leg.

"That's all it needed," he said. "Steady as a rock now."

He wiped his face with a filthy handkerchief, then he opened the stove's doors, crumpled a piece of paper, put it inside and lit it. It flared up quickly, then died. All the smoke went up the flue. "It draws beautiful. Really beautiful."

There was a pride of achievement in his voice which touched her, since the stove was not his own. "You deserve a beer for that," she said.

"I wouldn't say no."

She fetched a can, then poured herself a whiskey.

"Here's to the stove," she said. "Thank you very much, Mr. Leech."

"Call me Charlie," he said. "Everybody else does."

She said nothing and after a moment he began to roll himself a cigarette. He did it well and was utterly absorbed in what he was doing. She watched his big fingers, which should have been clumsy, roll the paper with the delicacy of a surgeon's. He was conscious of being watched. He raised it to his lips and licked it, then he held it out to her.

"No, thanks," she said.

"You ever tried one of these?"

She shook her head.

"Go on, try one."

She thought of his saliva on the paper. "I only smoke filter-tips."

"You don't get no taste with a filter-tip. Like having it off with a you-know-what on."

She ignored him, sorry now that she had offered another beer. He drank half the can in one gulp and said, "I wouldn't say no to a drop of whiskey. Just to take the dust from me throat."

Reluctantly, she poured a shot and said, "Water?"

"No water." He threw the whiskey back into his throat and chased it with beer. "Boilermaker," he said.

"I beg your pardon?"

"Boilermaker. Whiskey and beer." He stood by the fireplace with his elbow on the mantelpiece. The rain was lashing down but the thunder and lightning seemed to have moved away.

"Here," he said. "You got a sense of humor?"

"I hope so."

"You like a good story?"

Her heart sank.

"It's a bit naughty. But like they say . . . consenting adults. There was this sailor, see, and he's supposed to have the biggest—"

Just then Sophie began to cry. It was the first time Rachel had heard the sound with pleasure. "Excuse me," she said. "I must go. Thank you very much. I'll tell Mr. Chater to come over and see you tomorrow and settle up." Her tone was dismissive, final.

"Oh . . . all right, then."

"Good-bye, Mr. Leech."

She went upstairs. The wind had come up and was blowing half a gale from the southwest. She heard a door slam. Sophie was wet and very cross. Rachel changed her and stood at the window again, looking out at the storm. The rain was coming down in buckets, driven against the window by the wind.

As she put the baby down, she was suddenly tired.

Charlie had left a mess of brick dust in the sitting room. She picked up the beer cans and his whiskey glass and took them out to the kitchen. She was reaching into the cupboard for a dustpan and brush when she suddenly knew he was behind her. She had half-turned when she felt herself gripped from behind, hands covering her breasts. She was wearing a skirt and blouse and he began to pull the blouse out. The first impact of terror was overlaid by anger. She wanted to scream at him, to beat at him with the brush and pan. But part of her mind remained cool.

She stood stiffly as he fumbled with her bra, trying to put his hand underneath, and she said, "You'll tear my blouse, Mr. Leech, and that'll make some nice evidence for the police, won't it?"

He paused, turned her around and kissed her roughly. She tasted liquor and sweat and tobacco. "Come on," he said.

She raised her right hand. "Do you see these?" she said. He

looked at her sharp red nails. "You try to rape me and I'll rip your eyes out."

Her quiet voice and the coldness of the threat stopped him. He dropped his hands. "What makes you so particular?" he said. "It was only a bit of fun."

"Yes," she said. "Only a bit of fun. Good night, Mr. Leech."

She locked the back door after him, hating him for what he had done to her, hating him for putting her in a position where future meetings would be fraught with tension.

She went upstairs and brushed her teeth, while bathwater gushed from the taps. She swirled the toothpaste about in her mouth, cleansing her gums and tongue and lips of his smell; the bath would remove traces of his touch.

It was then that she first heard the tapping.

Tap. Tap. Tap.

She stopped and listened. It came again.

Tap. Tap.

Could it be a branch at the window? A door rattling? She went downstairs. The tapping was coming from the sitting room, where the light was on. And then she saw the face at the window: the black holes for eyes, the black hair plastered down by the rain and wind, the white knuckles against the glass. It was Charlie Leech. At this point, when she saw the blood running down his forehead and onto his cheeks, she screamed.

She stood, unable to take her eyes off him, and gradually regained control of herself. His lips moved but she could not make out what he was saying. Trembling, she opened a side window, too small for him to clamber through. He was soaked. The night outside was crashing with rain and wind.

"I rung the bell, but you didn't answer," he said. His voice was slurred and she saw that he had a cut just below the hairline.

"I didn't hear. What is it?"

"Can't get the van to start. I had the bonnet up but I can't see in the dark."

"What have you done to your head?"

"I caught it on a branch. You can't see nothing out there."

"What do you want me to do?"

"Could you give us a lift? I'd walk, only I'm not feeling too good." He indicated the cut and she realized he might be suffering from a mild concussion.

"It's only a mile down the road," he said. "Take you three or four minutes."

Still she hesitated. He must have known what she was thinking for he said, "Look, I'm sorry for . . . I didn't mean no harm." She realized that for a man like Charlie, who cultivated machismo with a naive assiduousness, the apology must have taken an effort.

"Wait there, I'll get a coat." She closed the window, went into the hall, and put on a raincoat and one of Bill's deerstalker hats. Her car was standing in front of the house.

"Which way?" she said.

"Turn right out of the gate."

They did not speak. There was no sound except the swish of the wipers.

"Next one to the right," he said.

She took the lane and drove on for a good mile. "Are we nearly there?"

"Not far now."

But when, in the next few minutes, they did not reach his cottage, she began to get angry. She thought of Sophie in the empty house. She thought of her waking up and crying and no one there to answer her. She began to drive faster. She came suddenly on a bend and saw Charlie's foot move as though covering a brake pedal. But she drove well. The car hugged the shiny tarmac and she brought it safely around. A hill loomed up. She put her foot down and the car leapt forward. As she neared the top she saw a faint lightening of the sky above her and realized that a car was coming up the hill on the other side. At that moment she reached the crest, and in the same second, she saw the cat. It was sitting in the middle of the road, lit from the back, a huge shadow on the hedge. It seemed colossal. Automatically, she swung to avoid it. The wheels lost their grip and the car sheared away to its right, crashed into an ash tree, then swerved down the side of the hill and through a fence, tipping over onto its side. The seatbelt held her body, but her right knee lashed against the steering wheel.

Charlie had not worn his belt. Perhaps, she was to think later, that was part of the machismo. His head smashed into the windshield, bulging and breaking it. The impact reaction had then thrown him backwards and he had come to rest sprawled in a tangle of limbs. Shock and horror caused her to lose consciousness and she did not wake until she was in hospital.

"That's it. That's everything," she said out loud. She had smoked three cigarettes and had walked half a mile on the sitting-room carpet, reliving the events of that night. She was pleased with herself and experienced a sense of relief that she had managed to gouge each detail from her subconscious. She felt as though a great weight had been raised from her. She was exhausted, but it was a healthy exhaustion. She wanted her bed. She wanted to sleep. She did not even need a whiskey, so she poured her untouched drink back into the decanter.

She went to the windows and flung back the curtains.

There was the face. Dark holes for eyes. Black hair. White cheeks. She opened her mouth to scream and a hole appeared in the face. She realized it was her own reflection. She should have laughed at her own fright. She should have said, "Fancy being frightened of yourself!" Instead, she put her hands to her cheeks and turned away and all the euphoria was gone as she realized that fear had taken root.

Outside on the lawn the cat watched the bar of light cross the lawn as Rachel opened the curtains. It had come to the house again, searching for the food it had just found in the garbage can when the dog had started to bark, but it had been unable to dislodge the bricks Rachel had put on the lid. It was starving. Having easily eluded the dog, which was still wandering in the forest, searching for it, it stared up at the light, then melted away into the shrubbery like a dark ghost. It would have to search the roads. Now it would eat anything.

6

The telephone rang late in the evening, its bell strident through the silent house. For a moment Rachel sat, immobilized by irrational panic, then she went into the study to answer it.

It was four days since Bill had left and she was far from becoming accustomed to loneliness. The ringing telephone, a contact with the outside world, should have been a comfort, but it was not. It was an intrusion, an invasion from the unknown. She hesitated with her hand on the receiver. Who would be ringing her at this hour?

"Darling?" The line was so clear that she gasped, without thinking, "Bill! Where are you?"

"I'm ringing from Talini's. Are you all right?"

Her voice steadied. "Fine! You?"

"The same. How's Sophie?"

"No problems. How's the screenplay going?"

"Slowly. That's why I rang. There are too many interruptions here, so we're moving out. Tomorrow we go up to the cabin Talini's been lent. We'll be there for at least three weeks, and there's no telephone. I couldn't resist the chance to hear your voice before we left. You're sure you're okay?"

"Quite sure. You mustn't worry about us. I wrote to you this morning, but you'll be gone from L.A. before the letter arrives."

"I hoped you might have written and I've arranged for mail to be forwarded to the cabin. God knows how long it'll take, though, the post isn't what it used to be. I feel awfully cut off from you, and I miss you all the time."

"Me too."

"What's been happening?"

Don't tell him Nurse Griffin has left, she said to herself. Don't mention the cat. Keep quiet even about the dog in case he should suspect you're scared. Don't say anything to worry him.

"I had drinks with the Renshaws the night you left. Alec came in for coffee one morning. Oh, and I've met a nice woman who has moved into a cottage nearby. She came here for a drink."

She heard relief in his voice. "So you haven't been too lonely. Darling, must go now. Franco's waiting. We're leaving at the crack of dawn tomorrow. Write often, won't you?"

"Of course I will."

When she heard the click of the receiver being replaced she put her own down slowly, feeling that her last tie with him had been cut. She had comforted herself more than once with the thought that if things became unbearable, he was at the end of a telephone, that she could dial Hollywood direct and be talking to him within minutes. Now, for at least three weeks, he would be out of reach. She realized that she did not even know where the cabin was.

That night she had the dream again and awoke, sweating and shivering.

The next morning as she took Sophie around the drive in her carriage something near the hedge caught Rachel's eye, and she saw that it was the little stone statuette of a cherub that had held a birdbath. It had stood on the lawn near the gate ever since she had come to live in the house. But now it had toppled over onto the drive and the birdbath was smashed. The odd thing was that the head was missing. She searched the vicinity, but could not find it. How could such a thing have happened, she wondered? The statuette was heavy and no wind could have blown it over. With relief, she remembered Franco. He must have put his paws up, probably to drink from the bath, and pushed it. But where was the head? Suddenly, she remembered the "Welcome Home" sign. No animal had scrawled that message. No animal could have hidden the broken head. So who had taken it? She widened her search, finding nothing, but as she bent to push aside the branches of a straggling syringa she heard a hiss, and a black animal shape ran across the drive and disappeared beyond the gates. It was the cat.

All desire to search for the head disappeared. She limped back to the house as quickly as she could, pushing Sophie's carriage, and did not feel safe until she had slammed the door behind her.

The days merged with one another until a week had gone by, then two.

Apart from tradesmen, she spoke to few outsiders.

She ran into Celia James once in the village shop and found herself disproportionately glad to see her. But it was an unsatisfactory encounter. Celia was in a hurry and explained that she had dashed out for some essential supplies while she was waiting for a new builder to arrive at the cottage.

"It's been hell since—." She stopped short, but Rachel was able to fill in the gap: since Charlie was killed. "Anyhow, the Renshaws recommended this man from Lexton and he promised to come today. Couldn't give me a time, so I'm terrified of missing him. I'm so sick of living in a mess . . ."

She was backing toward her car and Rachel watched forlornly as she tossed her purchases into the back seat. As she drove away she leaned out the window and called, "See you soon! When I get this wretched cottage fixed you must come over . . ."

"I don't mind the . . ." Rachel began, then checked herself. She would cheerfully have visited Celia in a derelict barn for her company. Then, as usual when she felt tears threatening, she tightened her lips, told herself not to be so ridiculously weepy, and returned to the house, resuming her struggle to come to terms with her life.

She called the Renshaws one day, to ask them for a drink, but Moira, with patently insincere regret, refused.

"So sorry, Rachel dear," she said. "David's been off-color and I've got a million things to do at the moment, otherwise we'd have loved to, of course." Her voice lifted hopefully. "Perhaps when Bill comes home?"

"Yes," Rachel said flatly. "Perhaps."

Physically she was improving. She had seen her own doctor, who practiced in Addiscombe, and now everything, according to him, depended on her. If she did her exercises, if she took care,

if she did not put any undue strain on the leg, it would continue
to improve.

"It still aches," she told him.

Dr. Williams was a short, florid man with a brush of gray hair
who wore half-lens glasses and had a way of peering over the
top of them that disconcerted her. He had a slight Welsh accent
that normally she would have found musical, but he was brisk
and no-nonsense and had a reputation for being rude to patients
who he thought might be wasting his time.

"Of course it still aches," he said. "You're lucky to have the
leg at all." He made her feel as though she were malingering.
She decided not to tell him that twice since she had come back
from the hospital it had collapsed under her when she had inad-
vertently put it to the ground at a slight angle. The first time she
had pulled herself up on a chair, the second there was no chair
and Penny had had to help her.

It was, however, not the physical aspect of her life that bothered her, but the mental. Although she was an imaginative
woman, she had always remained on the cheerful side of in-
troversion. As a teenager she had greeted each day with enthusiasm and this habit had remained with her into adulthood. Now
when she awoke she was grateful for the daylight hours, grateful
to have Sophie and Penny and Franco. Each day shaped itself
into a parabola. As it strengthened, so did she, until she was at
her best around noon and in the early afternoon. But then, as the
light began to fade and dusk crept in across the Great Forest,
her spirits would sink.

Her fear of fear itself had begun to increase. She remembered,
all too vividly, her postnatal depression, which at the time had
seemed so overwhelming and so inexplicable. Then she'd had
Bill by her side. Now the prospect of a similar bout of melan-
choly, combined with this curious, growing fear—of being alone,
of nameless horrors that might never happen, even of, for God's
sake, a cat!—seemed always to be on her mind.

She found herself constantly listening for—and hearing—rus-
tlings in the bushes, and became familiar with the feeling that
eyes were watching her, which she had experienced for the first
time a couple of nights after Bill had left.

Each afternoon she would take Penny home and then come

back to the lonely house. She had a routine. First she would inspect all the windows, making sure they were locked, then the doors. Then she would draw the curtains and switch on the lights. Often she would have the radio on in the kitchen when she prepared Sophie's meal, and the television going at the same time in the sitting room.

Late one evening, she heard footsteps. For once, she had turned off the television set—on the three available channels there was a choice of a play set in the Glasgow slums, a quiz show, or talking heads. She was sitting, staring into the fire, thinking of Bill, wishing she could just close her eyes and, when she opened them, find that time had miraculously telescoped and he was due home tomorrow.

At first she did not recognize the sound. The silence had been broken only by the ticking of the carriage-clock on the mantelpiece and her own breathing. As it penetrated her mind, she froze in her chair. It was a curious, rapping sound, only just audible. At first she thought it was the old boards creaking, but by now she was familiar with the sounds made by the house itself, and these were different. She listened, the muscles at the back of her neck stiff with tension. Tap. Tap. Tap. She turned her head sharply to the window, wondering whether it was the sound she heard in her dreams. But this was softer, not at all like knuckles on glass. It was more like leather-soled shoes tiptoeing on an uncarpeted wooden floor.

Sophie! The thought of the baby alone upstairs brought her to her feet. Without conscious thought, she ran into the corridor, which twisted away from her, narrow and dark. She made for the stairs, switching on every available light as she went. At the foot she paused and listened. There it was again. It seemed to come from the kitchen. A burglar? She looked around. On the landing above her there was a porcelain umbrella stand holding three walking sticks; Bill liked to carry one when they walked together on the Downs. She ran up the stairs as silently as possible, but the old, sagging treads groaned under her weight. The sounds were magnified through the house. At the top, she grasped one of the heavy sticks, then hurried to the door of Sophie's room. The child was sleeping peacefully.

Suddenly she thought, Frighten him! Make as much noise as you can! Then get to the telephone.

"Who's there?" she shouted. Then, "Bill, there's someone in the house! Call the police!"

She went down the stairs, dragging her stick along the banisters to create the maximum disturbance, and stopped at the bottom. Nothing happened. There was no sound. No tapping. Nothing. A slight breeze ruffled the air, blowing a strand of hair back from her face. She shuddered. It was as though a cold finger had touched her.

From upstairs, she heard a wail. Sophie had been awakened by the noise of her descent. He, whoever he was, would know now that there was a child in the house. She ran as best she could through the passages toward the origin of the tapping. The corridors were empty. So was the kitchen.

But the door to the larder was open and the wire-covered window that let air in was flapping in the cold night breeze.

She felt sick with relief and reaction. Her imagination had created a situation that did not exist. She moved to the window and pulled it so it clicked against its frame. Was that the sound she had heard? In retrospect, she was not sure—but it *could* have been. Not footsteps, just a window hitting its wooden frame. Tap. Tap. Tap.

She secured the catch and went to Sophie. She rocked the child to sleep once more, cursing herself. She had become panic-stricken because she had heard an unfamiliar noise. She had never done such a thing before, had always believed she was not easily frightened. Now, it seemed, almost anything could frighten her. What's the matter with me? she thought desperately. Then: Is something *wrong?*

Of course not, for God's sake! It was the loneliness and the darkness that had momentarily caused her to panic. There had been no footsteps, no intruder. Tomorrow, in the light of day, she would look back on the episode and see it for what it was.

But tomorrow the day would fade and night would come again. By seven o'clock it would be dark. In a week or so the clocks would be put forward an hour and British Summer Time would give way to Greenwich Mean Time. There would be an hour's less daylight. Darkness would arrive at six and soon five, then four . . .

She did not hear the tapping again, and made sure each evening that the larder window was locked, but a residue of unease remained with her. Sometimes at night she found herself holding her breath, listening to the silence, knowing even as she heard tiny, unidentifiable sounds that they were figments of her imagination.

She spent much of her time writing to Bill, long, cheerful letters telling him about the minutiae of her life, about Penny and Sophie. In her second letter, running short of subjects, she mentioned the cat, but turned it into a joke. "I seem to see it everywhere," she wrote. "Or if not the cat itself, its goddamn traces. Bones and things. Spoor? Is that what they call it? You don't know a good White Hunter, do you, to go on Safari and shoot the darn thing for me?"

And again: "The stove is working beautifully. You'd love it. It's so cozy. I have my drink in front of it. That's when I miss you most, my darling. So I have two drinks. One for me and one for you."

And again: "I told you about Penny in my last letter. Sophie has fallen for her like a ton of bricks. She seems to prefer her to me. I suppose it's all the crackers. She's getting plump. Her hair isn't spiky any more. She doesn't look like Chairman Mao. Penny thinks she is beautiful, and so do I."

She took a long time writing the letters. The hours passed in total concentration, without any unease about what the night might bring. And because she had been thinking more and more about America, she decided to start a short story. She wrote for three days and gradually the influence of work took hold of her and she found she was not brooding so much.

But when she read over what she had written, she was not satisfied with it. Her central character was a woman who had been left by her husband and who lived alone in a remote house on the New England coast in winter. The story dealt with her thoughts, her longings, and her fears. It was too subjective, too depressing. She tore it up.

She had letters from Bill, which she read and reread. He described Talini's Hollywood baroque house, with its pool and tennis court, its manicured lawns, its fountain, its garden lights, its gas barbecue, and its sauna. He made fun of it, but to Rachel, brought up among the fakery of Southern California, it seemed to be infinitely desirable. For a whole morning after reading the letter she could see in her mind's eye the gardens and the sprinklers of her youth and smell the scent of water on warm earth.

Her life became split into two: the good days and the bad days, and these largely depended on the weather—and on whether or not she saw the cat. As she had said to Bill, it seemed to be haunting her. Often, when she looked out of her window in the morning, she would see, or imagine she saw, a dark shape slink into the cover of the bushes. Once when she opened the front door, the branches of the rhododendrons were shaking, although there was no wind, and she knew the cat was there, somewhere, watching her.

Many of the trees around the edge of the paddock had lost their leaves; others retained them and the frosty nights had brought out the colors, every shade of brown, oxblood, and gold. On days when the sun shone the woods seemed to have an inner fire that burnt in its rays. On such days she would take Sophie and Franco for walks along the lanes or she would drive carefully to the top of the Downs and sit in the car while the dog chased birds. She felt safe with Franco, knowing, when they returned home as dusk fell, that he would scent the cat if it was around, and chase it away. Almost without realizing it, she had come to love the dog, and depend on his companionship.

Sometimes she would drive to the beach, deserted now at the beginning of winter. It always reminded her of the coast near Nantucket: the lonely sands, the low dunes, and the sea grass bending in the wind. On such days her fears would vanish. She would do her chores quickly and go out into the garden and prune the shrubs, or cut back the raspberry canes as the dog raced around the garden or lay quietly in the drive. On most days, even those without sun, she would put Sophie in her carriage in the sheltered angle of the house and the baby would sleep away the morning deep in her warm blankets but breathing the clean country air by which Rachel set such store. It had become a substitute for the cleanliness and health-giving force of the sea.

It was on one of the good days that she decided she felt strong enough to see Charlie's widow, but the experience was even more dreadful than she had anticipated.

The Leeches lived in a cottage, a rural slum with a rusting car squatting in the garden. Alongside a pathetic attempt at vegetable growing, a lopsided wooden gate opened onto a muddy path. The front door was in need of paint where children had kicked it and dogs had scratched at it.

Mrs. Leech must have been about Rachel's age, but looked at least ten years older. She had the careworn, lined look of a woman who has had too many children in too brief a period without the resources to cope. She stood in the front doorway carrying a baby in one arm while a little girl of about five clutched at her skirts.

Rachel could feel her heart pounding as she faced her. "I'm Rachel Chater," she said. "May I come in for a moment?"

Mrs. Leech made no move. She had probably once been pretty. She had long dark hair held back by an elastic band. Her eyes were light blue but they had a faded, exhausted quality and had sunk deeply into her head. Her hands were bony and red and the skin was pitted with dirt.

"May I come in?" Rachel repeated.

"What for?"

"To talk."

"What about?"

"I think you know."

"You killed Charlie. That's all there is to say."

Rachel had not expected this. She had not known what to expect: tears, hysterics, perhaps. But not this, and she shrank under the steady stare of the woman's blue eyes.

The little girl suddenly pushed her face forward and shouted, "My daddy's dead! My daddy's dead!"

"Shut up!" her mother said.

"Can't we go inside?" Rachel said. "We can't talk here."

Mrs. Leech gave ground and she stepped into the tiny cottage. With a nod of her head Mrs. Leech indicated that she should go to the right. The sitting room was a mess. There were papers and toys on the floor and the three-piece living-room set, which was covered in a furry material patterned to resemble a tiger skin, had seen better days. Net curtains, yellow with age, hung askew over the small windows. One wall had been papered to look as though it were built of mountain stone and in the middle of this was the fireplace, in which a small coal fire was burning. A clotheshorse on which were drying a dozen or more diapers stood in front of it. The smell of them permeated the house.

"May I sit down?" Rachel said, and then discovered that there was almost no surface that was not covered in toys or papers.

Mrs. Leech did not reply. She stood in the middle of the floor clutching the baby. The little girl flung herself into one of the chairs and began to kick it with her heels. The baby began to cry. Seemingly without conscious thought the woman reached into her dress, pulled out a breast, and allowed the baby to suckle. Like the rest of her, the breast was worn with too much use.

My God, Rachel thought, no wonder Charlie couldn't keep his hands off other women. There was something pathetic about Mrs. Leech; equally there was no doubt that she could not cope —with the house or with her family. At any other time Rachel might have felt sympathetic to so obvious a loser, but now she felt repelled by the dirt and the poverty and the hostility.

"I've come to say how sorry I am, and to ask if there is anything I can do for you," she began quickly. Get it over with, she told herself. Get it over, and get out.

Mrs. Leech stared at her, unembarrassed by the loud sucking noises coming from the baby. What more could she say, Rachel thought? She *was* sorry. But how do you say, I'm sorry for having killed your husband?

Mrs. Leech spoke: "You're sorry. Is that it?"

"Desperately sorry."

"Who for? Me or you?"

"You, of course. Why should I—I mean, yes, *I'm* sorry. We're all sorry."

"So you come here to get it off your chest, like. You think you can come and say, I'm sorry for killing Charlie, and that does it. That makes it better."

"I don't think like that at all! Nothing I can say will make it better. I know that. But I couldn't not come."

"You sure you didn't want to come just to see, like?"

"See what?"

"Me."

"Of course that's why I wanted to come. I wanted to see you and tell you . . ."

"I didn't mean it that way. I mean *me*. Charlie's wife. You think I like being left behind? You think I wanted Charlie dead? You know how many kids we got? Not *we* anymore. I got to remember that. You know how many kids I got? There's three more at school. That's five. What do you know about keeping five kids? You think you can come into somebody's life and walk away when you want to. It's always the same with you people in the big houses. You *used* Charlie!"

Rachel could see anger mounting in her face, but she did not know how to reply, so she stood there, thinking it better that the other woman should have her say.

The little girl sprang out of the chair. "Can I have a sweet?" she said.

Her mother ignored her. "He done everything for you. He done your houses. Decorating, painting, making them look nice. And look what we live in. You think I like living in a place like this? See that?" She pointed to a corner of the room where there was a large stain on the wallpaper.

"That's damp, that is. You come through here."

"Mrs. Leech . . ."

But she was beyond hearing. "Come on!" Rachel followed her into the kitchen.

"Look at that. Go on, look!" This was an appalling room, dark and fetid. An old porcelain sink and wooden drainboard were piled high with breakfast dishes, perhaps even yesterday's dishes as well. The table had not been cleared and there was half a stick of margarine, still in its paper, covered with raspberry jam and peanut butter where knives had scooped at it. "See?"

Above the sink the plaster had come away, leaving another festering area of damp.

"Do you have places like that in your house?"

"No," Rachel said.

"No. Because Charlie fixed them up. But he never fixed up his own home."

"Mum! Mum, can I have a sweet?" The little girl tugged at her skirt and Mrs. Leech slapped aimlessly at her.

"You shut up, you." Then to Rachel: "Charlie never had the time for us. Sometimes he never came home in his dinner hour. Sometimes not till eight or nine at night. It's not fair."

Doesn't she realize *why?* Rachel thought. Doesn't she know what a womanizer he was?

"Mrs. Leech . . ."

"And now you come here! Why? You say you're sorry. You weren't sorry for us when he was alive. You think I don't know? You tried to take Charlie away from me!"

"That's not true."

"You wanted Charlie for yourself. You think I didn't know? You can't live with a man like Charlie and not know. I could *smell* a woman on him!"

"I swear to you . . ."

"Get out! I want you to get out!"

"Mum . . ."

"Shut up! Go on! Get out of this house!" She was shrieking now, her face red. Rachel knew there was no way of making contact with her.

So the good day became a bad day, and there were other days when the house was enshrouded in mist, when a low, dark gray curtain of cloud filled the sky, when the winds raged through the Downs, bringing rain hissing off the sea. Those days she found difficult to endure. Sophie's crying would irritate her, and often she would go to Bill's garden room to escape. When she came back she would usually find Penny in Sophie's room and the baby would be gurgling with delight. And this would irritate her, too. She found herself becoming jealous of Penny. She had told Bill she thought Sophie liked Penny more than her. She had meant it as a joke, but there was an underlying truth. There was no doubt that Penny had a way with babies. What annoyed Rachel was that she seemed to spend more and more time with Sophie and consequently the house began to wear a neglected look. Dust accumulated on tables, the windows needed cleaning, stains began to appear in the bath.

One day she and Penny had a row. It started innocently enough on a day that was neither one thing nor the other. It had been sunny early, then the clouds had built up. Rachel had decided to take Sophie for a walk, but by the time she had finished her chores the sky had gone dark and was threatening rain. She had been looking forward to getting out so she decided to go anyway. She woke Sophie, zipped her into her little jumpsuit, and was carrying her downstairs when Penny appeared and said, "It's coming on to rain."

"I don't think so."

"Oh, but it is." There was something about the tone, the knowing, experienced tone of the local talking to a foreigner, that irritated her, and she said sharply, "I'll decide what we do, thank you, Penny."

She was aware of hurt on the big moon face but she did not care. She put Sophie in the carriage and walked down the drive. By the time they reached the gate the first spots of rain began to fall and she knew that if she went on they would both be drenched. Angrily she turned and as she did so she saw the body of the little statuette half hidden under the hedge.

She had managed to put the headless cherub out of her mind. After she had first seen it, it had formed part of her dream. Sometimes she would see its head without the body, at others the severed neck on its little shoulders, like some Greek statue mutilated by centuries of passing time. "Kids!" she said to herself. She saw in her mind's eye the placard: "Welcome home— you bitch!" "Goddamn kids," she said again.

The rain was coming down hard and she hurried up the drive. Penny met her at the door.

"I'll take Sophie," she said. Her face was guileless. There was no satisfaction about being right, but Rachel's anger, mixed with the shock of readmitting something unpleasant to her conscious mind that had been relegated to her subconscious, caused her to flare up.

"For Christ's sake, get on with your work!" she said.

"I've finished."

"Finished?" Rachel's voice rose. "You've hardly started. What about my bathroom?"

"I've done it."

"That's a lie. It wasn't done before I left with Sophie and you haven't had time."

A confused look came over the girl's face. "I thought—"

"You're always lying! You say you've done things and you haven't. You say you'll do them and you never do."

Penny burst into tears and ran into the back of the house, slamming the kitchen door behind her.

Rachel took Sophie upstairs and put her in her crib. She was shaking with the reaction to her sudden loss of control and knew she had to apologize to the girl. But when she came down again, Penny had her coat on.

"Where are you going?"

"I want to go home."

A chill came over Rachel. "You mean you don't want to work here any more?"

The eyes were puffy and tears still shone on the round, doughy cheeks. "You don't want me here."

Rachel had a picture of the house empty by day as well as by night and she felt panic rise. "Why do you think that?"

"The way you talked to me."

"Oh, Penny, I'm sorry! I came down to apologize. Honestly, I don't know what's wrong with me these days. I guess it must be because I'm alone so much." She fumbled for the right words to make the girl understand. "Sometimes I don't think I can bear this house any longer! Oh, hell . . . that's stupid, isn't it? I have to bear it. It's my home. Penny, please don't leave."

She held her breath as the girl stared at her, then exhaled in a long sigh as Penny nodded.

"Look, let's go and have a cup of coffee." She put her arm through Penny's and they went into the kitchen. She made them a cup of coffee and induced Penny to take her coat off and put her apron back on. By the time they had finished the coffee they were smiling at each other and a new understanding of their needs had become apparent: Rachel needed Penny just as much as Penny needed Sophie.

"All forgotten?" Rachel said. She was talking as she would have talked to a child.

Penny nodded, smiling through eyes that still glistened.

"Don't take any notice of me when I talk like that, because I don't mean it," Rachel said. "Now, are we friends again?"

"Yes. Except—"

"Except what?"

"What you said about me fibbing and all. Sometimes I think I do. Sometimes I can't help it. Sometimes I—I forget."

"We all do."

The dog began to bark and she looked out of the window. It was the postman. Franco ran down the drive to meet him and then lay at his feet and rolled over. The postman bent down and tickled his stomach. So much for the great guard dog, Rachel thought as she fetched the mail. There was another letter from Bill.

She went to his room to savor it in isolation, but it did not cheer her as she had hoped. The screenplay was going more slowly than he had expected. He and Talini were living comfortably enough in their cabin surrounded by great redwoods, visits from the occasional tradesman their only communication with the outside world. But Talini was proving a difficult collaborator and scene after scene had to be reworked. "So it looks now as though we will be here an extra month at least," he had written. "By that time the damn thing should either be finished or we'll be at each other's throats."

An extra month. Rachel sat, staring at the letter. It was to have been six weeks. Now it would be ten. Ten weeks by herself in this isolated place. Seventy lonely nights, seventy days and nights knowing that somewhere, outside, the cat was crouching, watching her, and there was not a damn thing she could do about it.

7

As the days shortened and winter tightened its grip on the old kingdom of the South Saxons, and light snow powdered the tops of the Downs where once only the iron-workers and the charcoal-burners had lived their fearful lives, her fears began to be concentrated on one particular time: when she switched off the light and tried to compose herself to sleep. She was able to get through the days and even the early evenings. The house then was full of the noise of Sophie and radio and television, and even though it was isolated in its forest clearing she had an impression of people and bustle and things happening around her. Sometimes she watched television until the station closed, before facing the staircase and the still rooms upstairs.

For two and three nights together she would go to sleep quickly, her book falling onto her chest, perhaps even with the light still on, and wake the following morning after a dreamless night. On others she would find it difficult to sleep at all and once having dropped off would wake at three or four in the morning, her mind filled with the just-out-of-reach horrors of dreams she could not recall. She would lie awake listening to the night noises—the creakings and groanings of the house—and she would tell herself that they were all explicable, that they were caused by the contraction of timbers in the roof. Sometimes she would hear the shriek of an owl or the bark of a fox or the scream of a wild animal dying violently and she would tell herself that these, too, were natural. But there were other noises close to the house: scrapings and scratchings for which she had no explanation. They could not be caused by Franco because he was in his basket. They sounded like claws on wire or someone rubbing a hedgehog against fine mesh. She knew of no circumstances which could cause such noises—but all the time, in the back of her mind, she was remembering the cat.

Often, lying in the big hard bed, she would long for Sophie to wake and cry so that she could pick her up and talk to her and comfort her. But Sophie did all her crying during the day and slept at night like the dead. There was one simple way, Rachel knew, to overcome her dread of the night, and that was to take two sleeping pills and anesthetize herself until dawn. But it was the one thing she could not do, for she also knew, from the infrequent times she had taken pills before, that she became totally unconscious and would never hear if her child were in distress.

And so she tried the only other method: physical exhaustion during the day, followed by alcohol in the evening. She would help Penny in the house, she would go for walks whenever the weather was good enough. She even began to use Bill's exercise bike, which he had bought when he thought his weight was going up; anything, as long as it made her tired. In the evening she would have a couple of whiskeys and a glass of wine or two with her supper and a whiskey before she went to bed, which often sent her to sleep quickly. But at other times it had the effect of waking her with a full bladder in the early hours of the morning, thereby defeating its purpose.

It was on one of her walks that she went to see Alec Webb. She had been feeling guilty about him, but his cottage lay at the end of a narrow, muddy track closed to cars and on which it was impossible to wheel the carriage. On a day of light drizzle she left the baby with Penny and went through the woods to the cottage. She found it in darkness. For a moment she thought he might be out; then she noticed that the front door was open. It was more isolated than her own house, a small thatched cottage that had been built at the end of the eighteenth century to house laborers and now, in the twentieth, had become "period" and expensive. It was beautifully kept, the garden was neat, the climbing roses still had a few flowers, and despite the fact that it was winter the lawn in front looked as though it had been newly cut.

She banged on the knocker. "Are you there, Alec? It's me, Rachel."

He came to the door, looking pleased. "Come away in, as my madam would have said." She gave her cheek to be kissed, remembering that Alec's wife, Mary, had been Scottish. He led her into the sitting room, switched on the lights, and drew the curtains. "That's better," he said. "Bloody day, isn't it? Now, what's it going to be, tea or a glass of wine? I've just been bottling some rather good rosé. First-growth Lexton."

"That's no contest," she said. "I'll have the wine."

"Good. Been looking for an excuse to get stuck into it myself." He bustled out on his short, jockey's legs. The room was spotless. It was decorated in chintz, with old beams, some good pieces of furniture, and a few antique saddle brasses at the sides of the fireplace.

He came back with a bottle and two glasses. "Tastes rather peach-flavored. What was it Thurber said? 'A naive domestic burgundy'? Well, this is a naive domestic rosé and you will certainly be surprised by its presumption, because I reckon it's stronger than normal wines."

He held the wine up to the light, swirled it in the glass, and said, "It's got a good color. I've often regretted that I didn't discover wine-making when my madam was alive. I think she would have enjoyed making the hedgerow wines." The light struck his patchwork face and his rigid glass eye and again Rachel experienced the slight shock of his appearance.

"What's the news?" he said, sitting down in an armchair opposite her. They talked about the weather and Bill and village topics for some minutes while he fidgeted with the smoldering fire, which he finally blew into life with a bellows. He said, "I'm glad you've got young Penny Mason working for you. I know her from Addiscombe. They're a good family. Now, how's the leg?"

"So-so." Then she said, "Alec, do you know anything about cats?"

He laughed, his good eye crinkling up, the glass one staring fixedly at her. "Vets are supposed to know something about cats."

"You remember I told you the accident happened because I swerved for a cat?"

"Yes, it was that feral cat, wasn't it? Curious thing is, I've never seen it."

"You couldn't miss it. It's bigger than an ordinary cat. And it has a wide face with marks on its forehead. Sort of battered looking. Very dark fur, almost black, but not quite. You can see darker rings on its tail."

The intensity with which she spoke removed the smile from his face. "What about it?" he said.

"All sorts of things. I think the car hit it, Alex. I think I've damaged it in some way. It's limping."

"That's possible. Is that what's worrying you?"

"Not only that. It's just that it seems to be haunting me. I saw it the day I came back from hospital. And it's been around the house two or three times. Celia James has seen it in the drive. She didn't know what cat it was, of course, but I did. It's been after the trash. And it's been killing things on the lawn. I've found bones and fur."

"We used to have cats when Mary was alive," he said. "And a couple of dogs. But now . . ." He waved a dismissive hand. "Odd creatures, cats. Did some research on them at one time. I was going to write a paper, but I never got around to it. They have a very highly developed brain. Strangely enough, it's basically the same as ours. The only really big difference is that we have larger frontal lobes, memory areas and the part that controls speech: the parts in what's called the neocortex. Don't let the word scare you—it means the part of the brain that has developed more recently. But the old part, the more primitive part, is practically the same in cats and in humans. For instance, the area that controls movement and posture and balance. The really odd thing is that the limbic area, which is the center for emotions and sensation like sex and rage and pain, pleasure and hunger and fear and so on, is practically identical. So when people talk about anthropomorphism—you know what that is?"

She nodded. "Giving animals human attributes."

"That's it. Well, it's not anthropomorphic to say that the cat experiences emotions like we do. It does. Cats have the same brain center for the same feelings we have. Strange animals. You know, scientists have stimulated some brain sites with electrodes and turned docile tabbies into raging beasts that will attack anything that comes into range. Tiny hormone pellets inserted in the right place can bring a castrated cat back to full sexual vigor."

He poured them each another glass of wine. She wanted to hear more, but equally she didn't want to. She listened with a kind of dread fascination.

"There's a curious irony about the cat." Alex was well launched now. "It mightn't exist in Western countries at all if it hadn't been for the rat. In the Middle Ages it was on the way to extinction. The Church outlawed witchcraft, and cats, of course, were associated with witches. One of the popes, can't remember which, encouraged the destruction of cats because they were looked on as such powerful allies to the witches."

Stop it, she wanted to say. *Stop it.*

"Witch-hunt really came to mean cat-hunt. And they were often burned and drowned with their owners. Punishment for sheltering a cat or caring for a sick cat could range from torture to burning at the stake. And then along came the brown rat and with it bubonic plague, and the cat became the first line of defense. So you see, the cat hasn't much to thank us for. In fact, you could say that of all the domestic animals it's suffered most at our hands. Are you all right?"

"Yes."

"But *your* cat—"

"It's not my cat!"

"No, but you know what I mean. It's a feral cat and that's something rather special: a domestic cat that has reverted to a state of wildness, hunting its prey just as a lion or a tiger would. And like a wild animal, it has a territory and a home range, which consists of places for resting and watching and sunbathing and a network of paths and a den—are you sure you're all right?"

Rachel had risen abruptly to her feet. The wine was making her dizzy. "I must go," she said thickly.

"Hang on a tick. I'll get my coat and come with you."

"No." She didn't want him with her, she didn't want him to tell her anything more. What he had said was disturbing enough.

All the way home through the darkening woods she looked out for a black shape that limped on one of its hind legs, but she saw nothing. That night as she lay awake with the light on she heard the scratching again. She remembered what Alec had said about the cat's brain, its rages, pleasures, and fears. Could it also experience an emotion like the need for revenge? What if it was trying to get into the house?

It was.

It crouched at the cellar window and scratched at the wire mesh, trying without success to pull it out of the way, for from the inside of the cellar came the smell of food.

There was a time when the cellar had been the coal-hole, with a door opening onto the backyard. But the door had been bricked up and a wooden chute fixed below the single window so that trucks could drive to the rear of the house and the coal-men could make their deliveries by tipping their sacks down the chute. In the late nineteen-fifties coal had given way to oil. The cellar had been cleaned and an oil-fired boiler installed. Since the cellar had only one small window through which the coal had been tipped onto the chute, and since fumes from the boiler were said to be dangerous, the window space had not been glazed, but covered in wire mesh. This allowed in air but not rats and mice. The mesh served as no real protection against burglars, so three iron bars were cemented into the window frame. As an extra safeguard the door from the cellar into the house could be bolted from both sides.

When Bill had bought the house the cellar was full of junk but Rachel had cleaned it out, distempered the walls, and put down linoleum. Then she had installed a big freezer chest and a tumble dryer. She had persuaded Bill to put up a series of shelves, which she used for storage. They held cartons of toilet paper and paper towels, bags of salt, boxes of detergent, and an array of canned food, as well as bags of dried fruit, packets of shelled walnuts and slivered almonds, a smoked ham, bags of flour and sugar, and a dozen pots of homemade raspberry jam.

It was the smell from these shelves rising on the cellar's warm air that had attracted the cat. It had come across to the house at night three or four times in the past fortnight, but each time the wire mesh had proved too much of an obstacle.

It was in constant pain now. An infection had set in around the splintered bone in its paw and it no longer tried to hunt. Instead it ate what carrion it could and rested for long periods in its den. The result was that it was on the edge of starvation. Its range had been more circumscribed as the pain of movement increased: the den, the paddock, and the Chaters' garden formed its world. And in the middle of this world was the house. In all its adult life it had never been inside a house. But briefly, as a young cat, it had lived in one. That had been on the outskirts of Addiscombe, when it had belonged to a woman known as Old Miss Mulgrave. It had been one of the Heinz cats, as the neighbors described them, for Miss Mulgrave had once called them her fifty-seven varieties. She was exaggerating, for at that time she had only seventeen cats. There were to be more later, until the total rose to thirty. The one that came to be the feral cat was a latecomer. Its father was a black tom, its mother a bigger-than-ordinary tortoiseshell, and it had spent its first few months with the horde that inhabited Miss Mulgrave's house.

Apart from some deliverymen, few people ever saw the old woman. She had wire mesh put over the windows of her house so she could leave them open in summer, when even she became aware of the smell, but the cats could not get out. In effect, she created a gigantic cage and, identifying herself with her cats, formed part of its imprisoned population.

As the years went by, her only contacts with the outside world were reduced to those whose services she could not do without. One was the local vet, Alec Webb. It was the usual practice in Addiscombe to take small sick animals to his office, but Miss Mulgrave always called him to her house. It was he who first noticed the deterioration in her.

"She looks like a Victorian engraving of a witch," he told his wife. "Thin as a beanpole, hair all over the place, always wears the same dress. I'll lay a bet she's got *anorexia nervosa* and if she doesn't watch out it'll kill her."

At four o'clock one afternoon Miss Mulgrave fell from her chair, striking the side of her face on the black cast-iron fender that surrounded the hearth. Two hours later, which was the cats' normal feeding time, they came in search of her. They found her on the sitting-room floor, still alive, but unconscious and bleeding from her ear and mouth. The cats mewed and arched their backs and raised their tails and rubbed themselves along her body, but she did not wake. With the black kitten, already the size of a normal cat, in the lead, they roamed the house, searching for something to eat. But all their food was in tins. For two days Miss Mulgrave lay on the floor as life slowly left her. At the end of the second day it flickered briefly, and then, like a shadow on the wall when the sun goes, it vanished.

At about the same time the black kitten approached the body warily and began to lick the half-dried blood. The experience stilled no pangs of hunger; on the contrary, the taste made it hungrier than ever, so it moved toward Miss Mulgrave again. The other cats followed.

"Christ, you have never seen anything like it!" Alec said to his wife. "The postman found her when he was trying to deliver her pension check. He phoned the police and they called me to deal with the cats. They panicked. A black one managed to tear down one of the wire window-screens and three or four got out. But the old woman . . ."

His wife refused to hear any more.

The cat was less than a year old when it escaped. It stayed in the wild and overgrown garden for some months, living on scraps it could forage from the dustbins of the nearby estate, and all the time it was teaching itself to hunt voles and mice and squirrels. But then the house was sold and bulldozers arrived and that was the end of the garden. The cat traveled through the woods, meeting other feral cats and avoiding their territories until it came to the wood above the Chaters' house. This territory was not already occupied and the cat dug its den and lined it with grass and settled down to its new life as a wild thing.

Now that life was over. The injury to its back paw made certain of that. The house at the end of the paddock was the cat's only means of subsistence and for the first time in its life it was trying to get *into* a house. It sensed that unless it could it would die.

8

It was nearly two weeks after her first visit that Celia James telephoned. Rachel had several times been tempted to call her, but she was unduly sensitive about revealing her vulnerability, especially after their encounter in the shop, when Celia had indicated firmly that their next meeting would have to be at her own convenience.

The telephone rang at half past six as Rachel was pouring herself the first of her evening drinks.

"Rachel?" The voice was warm, friendly. "It's Celia. Are you busy? I'm bored with my own company. I can't ask you here, because I'm still in a mess. Could I drop in?"

"I'd love to see you. Come as soon as you can."

She was surprised at her own pleasure at the prospect of Celia's company. She went around the sitting room, straightening cushions and magazines, emptying the ashtray. She set a couple of logs on the embers in the stove and stirred them into a blaze—and it was not until sometime later she realized it was the first time she had done so without seeing in her mind Charlie's face, dead in the flames.

The doorbell sounded and Celia was outside.

"You sounded surprised when I rang," she said.

"I was delighted."

"Didn't Penny tell you I called earlier? I waited for you to ring back."

"Penny didn't mention it. She tends to be forgetful. Come on in."

It was a damp, raw winter's evening and she had been feeling at her lowest. Celia stood in front of the fire, rubbed her hands, then turned, glancing around the room, appraising it. She was beautifully dressed, as usual, in a camel-hair coat, a white cashmere turtleneck sweater, Rive Gauche trousers with gold studs, and high tan boots with high heels. As usual, Rachel felt dowdy by comparison. Dressing carelessly was part of living by yourself, she thought. Whom did you have to dress for? And then she remembered that Celia also lived by herself.

Celia took a bottle of champagne out of the brown paper bag in her hand. "I thought we needed cheering up," she said. "I hate this damp weather."

The cork was difficult to remove. "We need a man for this," she said. "How's your husband?"

"Fine."

"So—absent friends!" She smiled over the rim of the glass.

The wine was ice cold and Rachel drank thirstily. Celia talked about village matters, a bring-and-buy sale in the church hall, the setting up of a fund to restore the church organ, and then she said, "How's your cat?"

There it was again. *Her* cat. "I haven't seen it for the past few days. But I have a feeling . . ." She paused.

"What?"

"I have a feeling it's . . ." She felt the skin on her scalp move and tears rose uncontrollably behind her eyes.

"What on earth's the matter?" Celia said.

"Don't take any notice of me—it's just that . . ."

"Can't you tell me?"

"I'm being silly."

"Look, I know what it's like to live alone. Everyone has moments like this."

"I know it sounds stupid but . . . it's that damned cat. I hit it, you see. In the car. And I've done something to its leg. And it sits out there." She waved at the black night. "Watching. Waiting. They've got brains, you know, nearly as big as ours. And they can feel emotions. It's trying to make me pay for what I did."

And then she told Celia all about the accident. It came pouring out in minute detail. She told her about Charlie and the woodstove, and giving him beer, and the tattoo on his arm. She told her how he had tried to rape her and she told her about going upstairs and brushing her teeth and washing and hearing the tapping. She told her about the rain and the storm and Charlie's face at the window. And then about how she had taken him home and had seen the cat, and swerved. She even described the dream.

"And now I hear scratching at night. It's the cat. At least, I think it's the cat. I feel as if it's trying to get into the house. Trying to get to me."

"My God, you really have been through it," Celia said. "It's only your imagination, you know. Has to be."

But even she, cool and practical, did not sound entirely convinced, Rachel thought. And Alec had made the cat sound so menacing, with his talk of limbic regions and witches, of raging furies and brain sizes.

"Let me pour you another drink," Celia said.

Rachel shook her head. "I've had enough. I'll get us something to eat."

"No . . ."

"Please! I wanted to call you. I wanted to say come over for an omelette. Now you're here, please don't leave."

They went into the kitchen and she mixed the eggs in a bowl. "How do you like yours?"

"Just with herbs. And runny."

There was a whine behind them and Celia turned. Franco was in his basket in the back passage.

"Do you think he wants to go out?" she said.

"He's been out all day. God knows where. He's taken to wandering all over the place. I worry about him sometimes."

"Dogs do wander. Bitches tend to stay around the house."

"He came in just before you arrived. He wouldn't touch his food. I figured he'd eaten something in the woods."

"How are you getting on with him?"

"I don't know what I'd do without him. He's just what I wanted, a companion. The trouble is, now he's settled down he gets along with everyone. He's all over the postman in the morning."

"I think I saw him earlier today."

"Where?"

"Up near the Renshaws. He was chasing a cat."

Rachel stopped what she was doing. "What sort of cat?"

"A dark one. I only saw it for a split second. Now don't get upset. There are dozens of cats around here. That's why dogs are put in the world, isn't it? To chase cats."

Rachel made the omelette and coffee and they took a tray back into the sitting room.

"How do you feel now?" Celia said.

"A lot better."

And she did. It is one thing facing a series of facts yourself, she thought, but quite another to share them. She felt as though a weight had been lifted from her. But this time there was an added emotion: gratitude to Celia for being there, for listening to her.

It was as they were finishing their coffee that Celia said suddenly, "One of the worst things must have been knowing you had to face Mrs. Leech."

"What? Oh, yes. It was the worst. It was terrible. She as much as told me I'd been sleeping with Charlie."

"How unpleasant." Celia poured herself another cup of coffee. "And had you?"

"Had I what?"

"Nothing. A joke in bad taste. But why did she accuse you, in particular?"

"I guess I was all she had. It was hysteria. But I've heard the rumors like everyone else. Charlie was the local stud, wasn't he?"

Celia said nothing, but tightened her mouth in distaste.

The big stove was burning brightly and the room, with its comfortable armchairs and sofas and its thick carpet, was an enclosed world. With Celia's company it was cozy, warm, familiar.

If only Bill were there, too . . .

"That's a marvelous stove," Celia said. "It warms the whole room. Where was it made?"

"Scandinavia, I guess. Bill bought it."

"Don't you find this climate ghastly after California? I've never been there, but I have a vision of constant sunshine and orange groves and suntanned people lying around swimming pools."

Rachel laughed. "It's like that often but it depends where you are—and on the time of year. Bill and I spent our first evening to-gether sitting over an open fire in a motel room."

"I didn't think open fires existed there. Where was this?"

"San Simeon, between Los Angeles and San Francisco. We'd met that afternoon at Hearst Castle, on top of a mountain . . . well, a hill, anyway."

"How romantic!"

"I suppose it was . . ."

Warmed by Celia's interest, and from a sudden need to bring Bill nearer, at least in memory, she found herself telling Celia about that first meeting, and the days that followed.

9

It had been romantic, she supposed. Not because it was on top
of anything, but because of the other circumstances governing
both their lives at that time. For her, it was an almost classic
case of rebound, and so she had been ultrasuspicious. The affair
she had been having with Michael had ground to a halt. Thinking of Michael brought California back: the heavy smell of the
sea, the ozone that made the evenings thick and salty, almost
creamy. They'd had an apartment almost on the beach.

He had been with Universal Studios then, writing movie and
television scripts. She tried to remember him physically, but his
image had faded. She could only recall a slight, gentle man who
wrote stories of violent action.

The apartment was beautiful, the surroundings were beautiful,
Michael was beautiful, she was beautiful, their lives were beautiful—but he was married. Only one thing to weigh in the balance against all the rest; it just happened to be the most important thing. She had lived with him for three years and the last
part had been dominated by his absent wife. On paper, Michael
could handle a four-car chase through the streets of San Francisco, a crazed gunman holding a child hostage in a New York
loft, or a dozen other epic struggles. But when his wife telephoned and said, If you don't come home I'm going to cut my
wrists, he went home, even though she had made the threat a
dozen times before.

That was how they lived; and who was Rachel to end it? You
go with a married man, you take the consequences. She had told
herself that over and over. Anyway, Michael had always come

back. A few days with . . . Martha, that was her name . . . a few days with Martha and the children and it was all over for the tenth or the twelfth or the twenty-first time.

She remembered their last Christmas. Everything was running slow for the week between Christmas and the New Year and she and Michael had decided to drive up Highway One, stopping where they found themselves, eating at the best restaurants, just getting away from Los Angeles, from Michael's wife, from all the hassle, and living for a while like the other beautiful people. Then on Christmas Eve the telephone had rung and it had been Martha. And Rachel had said, "If you go this time, I won't be here when you get back."

And he had said, "Sure," just as he had said the other times when she had threatened to walk out.

"What do you want me to do, let her kill herself?"

"You have to choose, Michael."

"You know exactly what I'd choose if I could."

"I figured I did. I don't any more."

"Listen, I'll be back day after Christmas. It's only one day."

"I'm telling you. I won't be here."

And so he had gone and she wasn't there when he came back.

She had spent Christmas Day packing. She thought of going to a hotel, but to be with but not part of the jollifications somehow would have made it worse. So she had stayed where she was and had not switched on the radio or TV, but had played Mahler's sad Ruckert songs most of the day and into the night. The telephone had rung three times and she had not answered it. Early the following morning she had left the sleeping city in her car.

Because she had once traveled with her father out into the Mojave Desert and because it was one of the things she had enjoyed most in her life, she took the same route: through Riverside and San Bernardino. There was snow on the San Gabriel Mountains. Even though she was early, there was a fair sprinkling of cars with skis on racks, all heading for the Sierra Nevadas. She reached Barstow at breakfast time, sunny and ice cold. She drove down the long main street and had, as she'd had when she had been with her father, a short stack of hotcakes with maple syrup and coffee, but it didn't do anything except make her feel she had overeaten.

She went on through Baker and then cut left into Death Valley and had lunch at Furnace Creek. The road was filled with campers. Everyone seemed to be laughing and enjoying themselves and she realized that this was not what she wanted. So she headed over Panamint Pass and stopped at a motel in Lone Pine. She could look out at Mt. Whitney through her bedroom window, a great rearing wall of snow and ice. Everything was still and clear and the air cut like a blade.

In brilliant sunshine the next day she drove back down to Mojave, then through Bakersfield and to the coast through Paso Robles, and spent the night at the Cavalier Inn in San Simeon.

They gave her a room overlooking the sea and a fireplace that burned logs of compressed sawdust and she stood on her balcony in the mild evening and looked at the sea and thought, This is what they had planned. She wanted Michael there, she wanted him to light the fire and open a bottle of wine and make love to her. Instead, here she was, looking out at the crashing waves with only the television set for company.

The following day was mild and sunny and she bought a ticket to see Hearst Castle. Built by the multimillionaire publisher William Randolph Hearst in the twenties, it was on a hill overlooking the Pacific. Her group of tourists seemed to be mainly Japanese. Their guide was a young girl with a spotty face and an arch manner.

They followed her past an outdoor swimming pool that Caligula might have designed, to what the guide called the "Casa Grande." She described the paintings and sculptures only in money terms: that cost a fortune, this was worth so many thousands of dollars, that was fabulously expensive. "And wouldn't it be a great room to play Ping-Pong in?" she said. Behind her, Rachel heard a voice say, "Christ!"

Much of the tour was like that, everything expressed in dollars, until they finally came to the great indoor swimming pool that had been built at a cost of millions and in which Hearst himself had never swum. The voice behind her, this time, she thought, speaking directly to her, said, "Imagine spending money on a thing like that in the Depression." She turned and looked up at a tall, mustached man, and realized he must have been behind her throughout the tour. There was something familiar about him. He looked at her, smiled, and said, "Hello."

"Hello," she said hesitantly.

"You don't recognize me, do you?" He had a deep voice and an English accent and was wearing black slacks and a dark blue shirt under a soft tweed jacket.

"I'm afraid . . ."

"You're at Paramount." She nodded. "I did *The Volcano* for you last year. Wrote it."

"Then you're . . . good Lord, you're Bill Chater!"

"And you're the lovely lady at the story conference."

"But you . . ." she began.

He touched his mustache. "It's new."

"What brings you here?"

"I've finished working on a script for CBS and I thought I'd see something of California before going home. And you?"

"Sort of the same."

They sat next to each other on the bus that took them back to the parking lot. "What did you think of it?" she said.

"Bloody awful. I've never seen anything so vulgar in my life."

"You mustn't be too hard on us. Remember there wasn't anyone building castles here in the tenth and eleventh centuries."

"I keep thinking of the millions of unemployed. The whole landscape was filled with men wandering about, penniless, and here's old Hearst beavering away at this ghastly monument, spending his money like water. It's a wonder they didn't lynch him. Maybe that's why he built it on top of a hill."

It was dusk when they reached their cars. "What now?" he said. "Which way are you headed?"

"I'll stay the night," she said. "I want to drive the coast route in daylight. And you?"

"I have a booking in Carmel."

She held out her hand. "I'll probably see you again on the lot."

"I hope so."

She drove back to the motel, had a shower, changed, and had just turned on the early evening newscast when there was a knock at the door. She opened it and saw Bill Chater. He had a large brown paper bag in one hand and a full ice-bucket in the other.

"Hi!" she said. "I thought you'd be in Carmel by now."

"May I come in?"

"Of course."

"I thought about what you said about seeing the coast in daylight. It makes a lot more sense than driving up in the dark. So I checked in here. And then I thought, wouldn't it be nice to have a drink with someone, and there's an off-license . . . I mean, a liquor store, across the road. So I bought these"—taking from the bag two long bottles of wine—"Crackling rosé, they're called. Iced. And I thought if you had a couple of glasses . . . *Do* you indulge?"

"I've been known to."

He gave her a tumbler of wine, poured one for himself, and said, "Isn't this nice?"

"Yes."

"I don't mean only the wine."

"I know what you mean."

They went onto the balcony and watched the waves and then he came back inside and lit the fire and they sat chatting and drinking. The phrase "like old friends" did not fit them at all, Rachel thought. They weren't old friends. And that was the nice part.

They had dinner together and the following day drove up the coast in tandem. She had planned to go through to San Francisco, but he said, Why not stop over at Carmel? Why not? She wasn't going anywhere in particular. So she checked in at the Jade Tree Inn and in the afternoon they sat on the beach on a mild gray day and watched the surfers in their wetsuits.

Again he came to her room and said, "It's the happy hour!" and again he had the iced rosé. Again there was a fire to be lit, and he lit it. Again they dined together.

And so it went on. He wanted to see the vineyards in the Napa Valley and she went to Yountville with him. Then they went to San Francisco and rode on the cable-cars and visited Pier 39 and Sausalito and did all the things the tourists did and by that time they were no longer taking separate rooms. She kept saying to herself, It's only an affair. I'm on the rebound.

But as the days passed she found herself less and less convinced by her own assertion until, finally, she was forced to recognize that she was in love with him. Michael had become a shadowy, unimportant figure in her background. With all his charm, he had been weak, vacillating, indecisive. Bill was strong and reliable; gentle, but with an underlying toughness; talented, considerate, amusing. Some nights she lay awake beside him, bleakly anticipating the day when they must part, the end of the affair. That was when she recognized that she did not want it to end. In a few short weeks he had become an essential part of her, and she knew that without him life would hardly be worth living.

Did he feel the same? She could not be sure and she told herself not to brood about it. It was too soon, anyway, for a commitment. They were both adults. They didn't *need* marriage. She had her job to keep her warm.

Her sturdy independence lasted only until he mentioned casually one evening that he had booked two seats on a flight to Mexico.

"That's nice. Why Mexico?" she said.

"We're getting married there."

"We are?"

"Of course. And don't tell me you haven't thought of it. We belong together. You know that as well as I do."

"Yes," she said, and felt suddenly dazed with happiness.

After that, everything went smoothly. Although she had enjoyed her work, she was no dedicated career girl and agreed without hesitation when Bill asked her if she would live in England. Apart from his deep love of his own country, he felt he worked better there than in the United States. Rachel had already visited Britain several times, had enjoyed life's gentler pace there and found that the natives, contrary to myth, were friendly, outgoing, and hospitable. In any case, she pointed out that as a free-lance writer she could work anywhere.

So they were married in Mexico and she never saw Michael again.

Because she had three months of a contract to work out, she had found another apartment and Bill had stayed with her there for five weeks, finishing his current novel. Then they had discovered she was pregnant and he had decided he had better precede her to England and find a house.

It took longer than he had anticipated, but after several weeks he wrote that he had found a place in Sussex. "It's a run-down old house, but with potential, I think," he said. "Anyway, if you don't like it, we can always move. It's in a particularly beautiful area. The house is about six miles from Addiscombe, a small market town, and Chichester (marvelous Cathedral, sixteenth-century market cross, Georgian houses—you'll love it) is the nearest city. I'm longing to introduce you to *my* places. Get moving, darling . . ."

So she had packed up and flown the Atlantic and moved into the gaunt pile that was to be her home, and now here she was, Mrs. Bill Chater, a mother, with a new country and a new life, normally as happy as a lark. Thank you, William Randolph Hearst.

Celia listened to the story with flattering attention and Rachel talked with increasing ease and frankness.

The only area that she did not touch, because it was, she sometimes thought, the one part of Bill's former life that had remained closed to her, was his first marriage.

He had told her, briefly, that he had married Sally when he was just twenty-one, and the marriage had been a failure. When she asked why, he had shrugged and said, "We were too young. Neither of us really knew the other."

"Did you and I know each other?"

"Enough," he had said. "And we're older."

"Tell me about Sally."

An expression crossed his face she had never seen before: closed, withdrawn. He had shaken his head. "It's in the past, Rachel. I've done my best to forget it. Don't make me rake it all over."

She had not persisted. There was a good deal she had not told him about her own relationship with Michael. Everyone had a right to the private areas of life. They had left it at that, and Sally's name had never been mentioned again.

It was eleven o'clock before Celia stood up. "I must go," she said. "Rachel, why don't we go up to London together one day? You could use a break and we could do some shopping."

Rachel was about to refuse, then she remembered that Penny would be delighted to look after Sophie.

"I'd love that," she said.

10

She slept more soundly and more securely that night than at any time since Bill had left; nor did she dream. She woke late and went immediately into Sophie's room. She opened the curtains and saw that the day was bleak and gray and the tops of the Downs hidden by mist. "We must hurry," she told the baby. "Penny will be waiting for us. Breakfast when we come back." As she put Sophie in her portable crib she remembered Franco, and called him. He was curled up in his basket, with his tail covering his face, and all she could see were his eyes.

"Don't you want to go out?"

The dog did not move.

She lifted the crib and went out the front door to the car, which was parked in the drive. As she hurried down the steps she felt a sudden spurt of pain in her right knee. The leg gave way. She tried to regain her balance, but the crib's weight pulled her forward and she sprawled down the stairs and onto the gravel. She managed to keep the crib upright. She had a moment of blind panic before she looked in and saw that the baby was lying on her back gurgling with delight at the novel experience.

She found she could not stand up. The knee felt like jelly. She sat on the steps and flexed it and massaged it until finally she regained her footing. The knee was sore, but it held her. Recently, feeling her leg was improving, she had begun to drive normally. She could do things that would have been impossible a few weeks ago. Then she'd had to pull herself upstairs on the banisters; now she was able to go up and down with relative ease. It was only these sudden collapses that worried her. They had something to do with abnormal displacement of weight. She assumed that eventually they would no longer occur.

It was nearly ten o'clock by the time she returned with Penny, and she took Sophie upstairs to feed her. She had just put down the bottle when Penny shouted. She heard running feet. "Mrs. Chater! Something dreadful's happened!" She felt a cold hand close over her heart. Penny was standing at the bottom of the stairs, her face creased with worry and fright.

"It's Franco!"

Rachel followed her into the back passage. The dog was curled up in the same position as she had left him.

"Look!" Penny pointed to the floor near the basket.

Rachel switched on the light and saw a dark pool of blood.

She bent down and stroked the golden head. The dog tried to raise it but he was so weak that all he managed was a few inches. She noticed that his tail, where it had been covering his mouth, was also saturated with blood.

"What's happened to him?" Penny said.

"God knows!"

She found herself wandering back into the kitchen. She stood in an almost catatonic stillness until Penny's voice brought her back to her senses.

"Are you going to phone Mr. Webb?"

"I'll fetch him," she said. "You look after Franco."

It took her less than ten minutes to return with Alec. He knelt by the basket, lifted the dog's head, then asked for a flashlight. She saw that Franco's blanket was soaked in blood.

"When did he come in?" Alec said, peering into the dog's mouth, raising his lips, looking at the gums and teeth.

"Yesterday afternoon. He'd been out all day. He wouldn't take his food. I figured he'd already eaten something."

"He had. He'd eaten Warfarin."

Rachel heard Penny draw in her breath. "What's that?"

"Rat poison."

"I didn't even think of that! I thought it was just a stomach thing from eating some trash he'd picked up in the woods and that he'd get over it. I didn't look properly this morning. He was all curled up with his tail over his face like he usually is."

"It's not your fault," Alec said. "And it's not the first time a dog's eaten Warfarin. Won't be the last, either. Bloody stuff."

"What can we do?"

"Nothing. It's too late."

"It can't be too late."

"He's dead."

The two women craned forward. "He can't be!" Rachel said. She put her hand on the dog's head, smoothing the short, soft fur. She felt a sense of loss which surprised her. Franco had given her a feeling of security of which she was now deprived, but it was not only that. She had been fond of him and had come to enjoy and rely on his company.

"It was a cruel way to die!" she burst out.

Alec shrugged. "I'm afraid animals have to endure a good deal of unthinking cruelty from humans," he said. "I want to show you something." He held the torch and pointed to a cut on the bottom of the dog's muzzle. The area around it was covered with blood. "That's what did it."

"But it's only a small cut."

"Warfarin's an anticoagulant. A rat eats it, starts to bleed internally, and goes away and dies. If a dog eats it and gets a cut or a bruise it simply bleeds to death unless it's checked. The blood won't clot, you see."

"Where could he have got it from?"

"Anywhere. Farmers use it. There's no problem about buying it."

They went through into the kitchen.

"He was seen up at the Renshaws yesterday," Rachel said. "He might have picked it up there."

"Perhaps. I'll call David." He spoke for a few minutes then put the telephone down. "He has Warfarin down in his corn store, in drainpipes. That's how they lay it out as bait, in cutoff drainpipes. It looks like a fine oatmeal and they put the pipes in corn stores. A rat can get into the pipe to eat it but the pipe is too small for cats or dogs. Sometimes the drainpipes get shifted and the poison comes out. I asked David if he had seen the dog up there but he wasn't home yesterday."

"What do we do now?" Rachel said.

"There's nothing we can do except bury him."

They buried the dog in an old rosebed, where the ground was soft, on the edge of the paddock. Alec found a spade in the toolshed and quickly and neatly dug a hole two feet deep and they put in the body, wrapped in polyethylene sheeting. He returned as much earth as he could, then placed several large stones on top of the grave. Rachel watched him, saying nothing, aware of the increased loneliness she would feel without the dog and at the same time guilty, despite Alec's reassurance, because she had not recognized the dog's distress earlier.

There was a strong smell of lysol in the house and Penny had removed Franco's basket. To Rachel, the place suddenly seemed very empty.

"Why did you put the stones on Franco's grave?" she asked suddenly.

Alec looked surprised. "Must have been automatic. It's what we used to do in North Africa when one of our chaps bought it. We'd dig a grave in the sand or in a wadi somewhere and put the body in and then place stones on top of it so the desert foxes couldn't dig it up and eat it. I remember once we booby-trapped a desk in a German officer's billet. Put the bomb in the bottom drawer . . ."

"I know why you put the stones over the grave," she broke in.

"I just told you."

"You put them there to stop the cat from digging up Franco!"

"Don't be silly!"

"You're lying!"

Her voice began to rise and Alec twisted his head so his one good eye was fully on her. "Look, Rachel, I swear to you I never thought about . . ."

"It's true! You know it's true!"

"I think you need a drink. We both do. Come on."

They went through into the sitting room and he poured her a stiff gin and tonic. "Drink that," he said as he helped himself to one. "The sun's not over the yardarm yet, but what the hell." He drank. "Now look," he said, his burnt-patchwork face trying to arrange itself into an expression of understanding and sympathy. "You're overwrought and I don't blame you. But let's analyze what has happened. Scores of dogs die every year from eating one poison bait or another. It's simply a hazard of keeping a dog in the country. Just as scores of cats are run over by cars . . ."

"He was with me all last night. I should have noticed something."

"He was out all day. He refused his food. That's not uncommon. You thought he'd eaten something which was making him sick. Just as Sophie sometimes feels sick or off her food. We all do. There's nothing uncommon about that. Nothing to make you suspicious."

"But he was bleeding all the time."

"All right. But he lay with his tail over his face—most dogs do, because they don't like breathing cold air—so you couldn't see anything. You can't blame yourself."

"Celia told me she'd seen him at the Renshaws. He was chasing a cat."

"For God's sake, love, get that cat out of your head! Nearly all dogs chase cats. And who's to say it was *your* cat?" There it was again, like a drumbeat. "Okay, the dog chases a cat, any cat. Perhaps it *was* the feral cat. Gets up to the Renshaws, goes into the corn store, the drainpipe is knocked over for some reason; he eats the meal with the Warfarin in it. He has a cut on his mouth. If it didn't happen just after he had eaten the poison it could have happened today or tomorrow. The effect would have been the same. Even a bruise would have caused him to bleed internally and that would have killed him."

"Alec, what if it wasn't a cut?"

"What do you mean, if it wasn't a cut?"

"What if it was a scratch?"

"I don't follow."

"Don't you see? The cat could have scratched Franco!"

"It's possible, I suppose." And then her implication dawned on him. "Wait a minute! Are you saying that the cat led the dog to the Warfarin and then deliberately scratched him?"

"Why not?" she whispered.

"Because it's preposterous!"

"You told me how clever cats were. You told me how big their brains were. How they think like us."

"Rachel, I meant they have similar instincts to us, given a similar set of stimuli. I didn't mean they can plan an entire campaign around killing a dog by luring it to eat poison and later scratching it to start uncontrollable bleeding. I've never heard anything so fantastic in my life!"

She sat there, staring at him. He couldn't understand. He didn't know the cat as she did. Nor had *he* ever harmed it.

"I once knew an old woman over in Addiscombe who lived with thirty cats. Total amity all round." He was talking for the sake of it, to give her time to collect herself. "I remember her name was Mulgrave. Old Miss Mulgrave, we used to call her. Lived all by herself in an old mansion with her cats. No one was allowed in except me; I was the vet, you see. She became odder and odder. Starved herself to death finally. No one knew for days."

"What about the cats?"

"What *about* the cats?"

"When she died, what happened to the cats?"

"Oh, my God—you never saw . . ." Suddenly he found himself floundering and finished lamely, "Some broke through a mesh screen on one of her windows and got out."

"You see," she said fiercely. "They *can* think. They *can* plan!"

The cat was working at the mesh screen over the cellar window, and this time it had some success. A section of the screen had started to rust years ago and by now had become weakened. A small piece of worn mesh, not more than a centimeter, came away. The cat felt it, and sensed the weakness. It began to pull at the place again with its claws and had soon opened a hole about the size of one of its paws.

Inside the house, the telephone rang. Rachel had been dozing in her chair and sat bolt upright. For a moment she was disoriented. She could have been in California, New York, London. But she wasn't. She was in the house in Sussex and she had to hurry through the dark corridor and pick up the telephone. Too muzzy to think of switching on lights, she groped her way blindly into Bill's study. He was ringing her from Los Angeles . . . it had to be him . . .

It wasn't. The line was open, but no one replied to her greeting.

"Hullo?" she said. "Who is it? Hullo? Is that you, Bill?"

There was no answer, though she imagined she could hear soft breathing.

After a moment, she replaced the receiver. She switched on the desk lamp and waited for a few minutes, but whoever the caller was, he did not ring again. She had always disliked the sound of a telephone ringing in the night and had to force herself not to run back to the cozy warmth of the sitting room. But even when she reached it, she found no comfort and she fought down a wave of irrational fear. Why would anyone have dialed her number, then listened to her in silence? Would they have known she was alone in the house? A memory rose to her mind of the night she had thought she heard footsteps and she found herself wondering whether the sounds really had been made by the larder window . . .

After a moment, leaving all the lights on, twitching the curtains to make sure there was no gap through which anyone could see inside, she went upstairs to bed. For some reason, it seemed safer upstairs.

11

This was escape. There was no other word for it. As the train rushed across the Sussex countryside Rachel felt she was heading toward a freedom from anxiety she had not experienced for a long time. She was leaving an incubus behind her.

She was on her way to London: sprawling, grubby, crowded, sophisticated London. A grown-up city where people were interested in a wider world, where she could be part of a bustle and excitement she had almost forgotten existed. For one day, she was escaping from the house in the clearing with its inexplicable noises, its jangling telephone, its dimly lit rooms and stifling walls. With every mile, her spirits lifted.

It was a bright, sunny, crisp winter's day. She and Celia were in a first-class compartment and had it to themselves. She felt the tension draining out of her as they chatted, to such an extent that when Celia said casually, "How's Franco? Is he fulfilling his guard-dog duties?" she was able to recount the story of his death. For the past few days she had not allowed herself to even think of it, for when she did, the specter of the cat—watchful, vengeful—rose before her. Now, in the train, her enclosed world receding, its menace decreased.

"You mean to say he simply bled to death?" Celia said.

"It was as simple as that. If I'd only noticed earlier we might have saved him."

"And you think it was the cat?"

"I know it sounds hysterical and I was feeling hysterical at the time, but isn't it uncanny? You saw Franco up at the Renshaws chasing the cat—"

"I didn't say it was the cat that has been bothering you."

"I know you didn't, but I'd bet on it."

"Let's forget it! Put it out of your mind, Rachel. No gloomy thoughts today. Pure enjoyment."

London was at its best. There were few tourists to crowd the streets and rain from the previous night had washed the air and the buildings so that everything stood out in razor-sharp relief. The color of the old brick was mellow in the sunshine, the new white buildings were golden, and the place had a serenity that Rachel associated with an earlier time.

She had not been shopping in London since long before Sophie was born. She had been planning a celebratory extravaganza once her figure returned to normal, but that had coincided with the accident. She was like a desert traveler who unexpectedly sees an oasis. As the taxi took her past the great shops, she thought she had never seen clothes look more beautiful, nor had she ever felt more lustful for them. Prices had gone up, but nothing was going to deter her. She told herself that she owed it to Bill to look her best.

The day was an expensive blur. At Brown's in South Moulton Street she bought a dark green velvet dress. At Ferragamo's in Bond Street, matching sandals with high heels. She knew she would not be able to wear them often with her knee in its present condition, but that would change. They went on to Janet Reger's, where she bought underwear and a nightgown: everything was silk or satin, lace-trimmed, with a feeling of luxury and a hint of decadence.

Then they went into a small shop in Bond Street where Celia bought an expensive handbag. As they were on their way out, she saw a frame of dress rings.

"Those are nice," she remarked.

"Aren't they lovely?" the saleswoman said. "Mexican silver and turquoise."

"Do you like them?" Celia asked Rachel.

"I wish I had the hands for them."

"I love chunky rings." Celia tried two or three and finally settled on one with a setting in the shape of a serpent. The stone was a single long turquoise. "I'll take this."

When they were outside she said, "Lunch. My treat. I've booked a table at the Ritz. Well . . . why not?"

"Sure. Why not." Rachel was feeling high for the first time for months and she had never been to the Ritz. They sat near a window that looked over Green Park. The sunshine had drawn people out of their offices and even in the cold some sat huddled on deck chairs enjoying the bracing air. Both outside and inside the hotel, everything sparkled. The cutlery on the tables shone, the napery was snow-white. It had been a long time since Rachel had dined in a smart London restaurant and she absorbed the scene like a schoolgirl, from the cherubs on the magnificent painted ceiling to the fine moldings, the great windows.

"This room is practically a national monument," Celia said, smiling at Rachel's unabashed delight. "In fact, it's listed by the Fine Arts Commission."

"It's beautiful."

"Let's hope the food lives up to its standard." A waiter in a black suit with starched white shirt gave them the menus. "Now, no holding back," Celia said. "You're not on a diet."

"Not yet!" Rachel said, looking at the list of dishes. "They've got *moules marinières*."

"I love *moules*. I'll have them, and I think I'll stay fishy. A sole. Grilled. Off the bone. I never get sole at home."

Celia nodded. "Make that two." From the wine waiter she ordered a bottle of Sancerre.

The room filled up. The women were casually elegant, most of the men formally dressed in dark suits. Rachel liked that; the restaurant would have been desecrated by jeans. "Bill's been here occasionally," she said. "His publisher brings him."

She ate too much and drank too much, but she didn't care. She was enjoying herself. The cat and the dark, enclosed valley in the Downs seemed a long way away.

"What about some strawberries? They're flown in from Kenya," Celia said.

"No. I'm going the whole hog. Rum baba." She had a rum baba and a Cointreau with her coffee and by that time her leg, which had suffered in the shopping, was no longer aching.

"It's been the nicest day I've had since Bill left," she said impulsively.

"It was too bad he had to go away when he did. How's the screenplay coming?"

"Okay, I guess, but it's taking longer than he expected, damn it. The time without him passes awfully slowly."

"Just be happy you'll have him back," Celia said. She was looking down into her coffeecup, eyes hooded. With her sleek dark hair and pale skin she looked like a madonna from a Renaissance painting.

"That was tactless of me. I forgot you had been married. You seem so marvelously self-sufficient."

"I've had to be."

Since Rachel had arrived in England she had all too rarely had a chance to indulge in woman-talk with a friend with whom she felt at ease, and she suddenly realized how much she had missed it. The combination of alcohol and euphoria at her release from responsibilities had melted away much of her normal reserve.

"I had a—an affair which lasted for a long time before I met Bill," she said. "When it ended I thought a part of me had died. I can't even imagine what it must have been to be widowed."

"Widowed. Divorced. The end of an affair. They're all bad."

"Bill was married before, years ago. Unhappily. He doesn't talk about it even to me. I often say a little prayer of thanks to Sally, though, because if the marriage had been a success I'd never have met him."

She became aware that Celia was staring at her. "Sally? Sally Chater? Where did she come from?"

"I haven't the faintest idea. Why?"

"I knew a Sally Chater up north."

"I wonder whether it could be the same one. What was she like?"

"To look at? Oh, tallish, good-looking."

"Dark or fair?"

"Middling. She lived in Yorkshire. She was alone, but she had been married. I'm sure she couldn't have been Bill's wife, though. It would be too coincidental."

"What happened to her?"

"She was an actress. She'd had a few small parts in British pictures, then I heard she'd gone to Hollywood. Perhaps she's still there."

Rachel sipped her coffee without tasting it. "But you don't think she could be the same one?"

"Probably not. Still . . ."

"What?"

"Nothing. She had a child, so she couldn't be. Bill hasn't a child by his first marriage, has he?"

Rachel shook her head. But would she know if he had?

"There you are, then. I remember she told me she and her husband had been crazy about each other."

"What was his Christian name?"

"Don't know. She always used some silly nickname. I can't remember what it was. Heavens, Rachel, it was years ago! Anyway, she can't be the same one."

Rachel pushed away the tasteless coffee; the view over Green Park had darkened. She knew, as surely as she knew that she was the second Mrs. Chater, that the woman Celia had known had been Bill's first wife. Who was now in Hollywood. *She had a child.* Why hadn't Bill ever told her he already had one child?

"Was it a boy or girl?" she said abruptly.

"Who? Oh, Sally's baby. I haven't the faintest idea. It's a long time since I knew her. I never saw the child."

She and her husband were crazy about each other. Why was Bill always so reluctant to talk about his first marriage? She wanted to go home, where she could think. She stood up.

"Time to go?" Celia said. "You were right, it's been a lovely day, Rachel."

On the train they again had a compartment to themselves. For Rachel, the day's magic had gone. Clouds were building up and the afternoon was beginning to fade. Bill and Sally. Sally Chater. Their child. Sally in Hollywood. Bill in Hollywood. And Bill had gone to a cabin in the mountains where, he had said, she could not contact him. But he was with Franco Talini, wasn't he? Or was he?

Driving from the station in Chichester back to Lexton, she felt tension mounting, and her urge to be home was mixed with dread. Another lonely night. The fear of fear. Fear itself, closing in on her, with the added burden of what she had learned about Bill and his first wife.

It was full dark by the time they reached the house. Penny came to the car to help with her packages.

"That's mine." Celia indicated one of the shopping bags. "Put it in my car, will you? Rachel, it's been fun. We must do it again."

"Won't you stay for a drink?"

"Well, just one, then I must go. I promised Alec I'd drop in for coffee later. He's a dear, isn't he? By the way, you haven't told me, what's the latest news from Bill?"

Rachel described Bill's most recent letter (was there anything he had *not* told her, she wondered) and they chatted desultorily about it and then about the Renshaws who, Celia said, were about to leave to spend the rest of the winter in Morocco. Although she found David and Moira bores, Rachel heard this news with a pang: her isolation, it seemed, was increasing. She had no dog and soon her only acquaintances in the vicinity would be Alec and Celia.

She watched the red taillights of Celia's car go down the drive and out of the gate. When she had driven Penny home she bolted the front door and went around the house, locking up. As she drew the curtains in all the ground-floor rooms she thought how vulnerable she was to watching eyes. From ground level outside even a child, on tiptoe, could see through the house. The back passage seemed bare and lonely without Franco curled up in his basket. I'll get another dog, she thought. And then: But what if it happens again?

She went into the sitting room, turned on the TV, and without thinking, poured herself a whiskey and took it to the big armchair near the fire. She was physically tired after the day in London and that pleased her, for she would probably be able to sleep. No matter how she tried to ignore it, the thought of Bill and Sally kept creeping into her mind. Why had he been so unwilling to talk about her? She had assumed it was because, as he had said, the marriage had been unhappy and he wanted to forget it. Could it have been, instead, that he had been so brokenhearted by its collapse that he could not bear to share his unhappiness, especially with his new wife?

She swallowed her drink and felt the first warmth spread

through her limbs. Automatically, she rose to pour herself another and, as she passed, glanced at herself in the gilt mirror above the fireplace. She saw a woman of thirty, her body still supple, breasts high and firm. But she was small, not "tallish" as Celia had described Sally. And she had never thought of herself as good-looking: the face under the auburn hair was less gaunt than it had been, but a shade too sharp for real beauty and there was still a shadow in the depths of her eyes.

The telephone rang as she was pouring water into her whiskey and her hand jerked so some drops splashed on to the carpet. She went into Bill's study to answer it.

"Hello?"

There was a jumble of sound at the other end. A voice said something, but too quickly for her to make out.

"What?"

There was a click as the line went dead.

She stood staring at the telephone. It had been a man's voice, but that was all she could tell. Muffled. Quick.

She returned to her chair and crouched in front of the television. The news ended. She finished her drink and switched off the TV. Bed, she said to herself. She did not want to think about the telephone call, either.

And then she remembered that she had not taken anything out of the freezer for the following day's lunch. She usually did this in the daylight hours because there was something about going into the cellar at night that she disliked. She opened the door and switched on the light. A flight of concrete steps led down. The single bulb only lit the cellar's central area and the corners drifted away into shadow. As she went down the stairs the domestic boiler was directly on her right. Opposite was the freezer chest and the shelves that she used for storage. Halfway across the floor she noticed that something had fallen from one of the shelves. She could make out part of a package. It was a large carton of mixed dried fruit, and some of the fruit had rolled out onto the floor. It must have fallen from one of the shelves and burst on impact. It was the sort of thing that would bring mice or, God forbid, rats, if it was not cleaned up. She moved forward, bent to pick it up, and saw the cat.

It was crouching in the corner where the freezer joined the

wall. It seemed huge. Its back was arched and some of its hair stood on end. Its mouth was open, showing the big incisor teeth. Suddenly it spat at her. The air hissed up its throat. She reared back and screamed, flailing her hands in front of her. The black mass on the floor launched itself upwards at her. She felt the fur on her face, covering her mouth, choking her. And the claws digging into her shoulders. Everything happened in a split second. The roiling, spitting body seemed to envelop her. She screamed again, fighting it with her hands. And then it leaped to the top of the freezer and she saw a black blur as it raced the length of the cellar, up what had been the old coal chute, and was gone.

She put her hands up to her neck. One came away with blood on it. She stared at it and screamed and screamed, her whole body shaking and shuddering. Then she turned and ran.

12

"And you say it was there?"Alec said, indicating the dark corner between freezer and wall.

It was the following morning and they were in the cellar. It seemed impossible to Rachel now that the incident had ever happened, yet there on the floor was the broken carton of dried fruit.

"It was feeding," Alec said, picking up part of a pear that showed marks of having been chewed. He held it close to his weak eye. "It must have been ravenous to go after this. You bent down?"

"Just as you've done. I bent to pick up the carton."

"And it went for you?"

"Yes."

She lit a cigarette and found that her hands were shaking so much that she could hardly bring the flame and the end of the cigarette together. Coming into the cellar had brought it all back.

"Poor thing must have been terrified," Alec said.

She laughed bitterly. "They say the English like animals more than people, don't they?"

"I'm sorry, I didn't mean it to sound that way. But it's true, isn't it?"

She tried to control the anger in her voice, but she was suddenly seething. "You didn't believe me!" she said. "And now you see what's happened!"

She had not slept much. After the attack she had closed and locked the cellar door and had gone upstairs to Sophie, picked her out of her crib and spent the night with the light on and the baby beside her. As gray dawn was beginning to lighten the room she dozed for a while; then it was time to get up and fetch Penny. She had told the girl nothing, but as soon as she had fed Sophie she had gone in search of Alec.

"You're making too much out of this," he said.

"Look!" She pulled down the top of her turtleneck sweater and showed him the scratch marks. "Is that all you can say?"

He flushed. But only in parts of his face. The grafted skin remained its normal brownish-white and, with his one good eye, gave him an alarming, blotchy appearance. "It was terrified," he repeated. "That's why it attacked you."

"It was *waiting* for me," she said flatly.

"Don't you see, you got between it and the window? It couldn't see a way around you. The freezer was hemming it in, the shelves were above it. You were in the way."

"It's easy to rationalize now. You weren't there."

"Listen, love, I think I can understand how you feel, but believe me, that cat wasn't waiting for you. It's far more terrified of you than you are of it. You've made it into a sort of monster, but it's only a cat."

"It *is* a monster," she said. "Look how it got in here. It just *happened* to pick on the weakest part of the screen?"

He took her hand and said, "I'm worried about you, Rachel. You've let this get you down. And really, it's all in your mind."

She heard echoes of her earlier thoughts: the fear of fear itself. She felt tears well up behind her eyes and she wanted to put her head down on his shoulder and let him comfort her as her father would have done. But it wasn't possible. You're a grown lady, she told herself, for God's sake act like one. She fought her emotions and said, "Alec, I want the cat killed."

"Have you thought of going about it the opposite way?"

"Which way is that?"

"It's clearly desperate. If, as you say, its paw is injured, it means it may not be able to hunt. It's searching for food. That's why it comes here."

"Well?"

"Why not give it food? Why not put food out for it?"

Her brow furrowed for a moment and then her face cleared.

"That's brilliant! We could put poison in the food." Out of the mists of her memory came a word. "Strychnine," she said. "We could put strychnine in the food."

His mouth turned down in disgust. "Wasn't Warfarin bad enough? My God, you want to see what strychnine does. I've seen animals die of strychnine poisoning. The convulsions are so great they've actually snapped their bones."

"That's what I thought you—"

He shrugged. "If you're that desperate, there's only one thing to do."

"What's that?"

"Shoot it."

"I can't shoot anything."

"I didn't mean you. I've got a shotgun up at the cottage. I'll shoot it."

"Would you really? I'd be so grateful. I know it's a dreadful thing to do but—it's just that . . ."

"It's probably in pain anyway, with that paw. Put it out of its misery. Save it from a lingering death."

She smiled for the first time. "Thank you." Then she remembered something. "What about the broken screen? Could you mend it before you go?"

"What do you want to mend that for? It's the one way we know it gets in. That's the place to shoot it."

They heard the door of the cellar open and Penny put her head around. "Mrs. Chater," she said, "Mrs. James is here."

"You go on up," Alec said. "I'll have a bit of a scout round."

Celia was in the hall and they greeted each other like old and intimate friends. Celia said, "I hope I haven't come at a bad moment?"

"You couldn't have come at a better one. Coffee?"

"Rachel, there's something I . . ."

"Come and have coffee first."

They went through to the kitchen and sat at the table. Rachel told her what had happened.

"You mean it was in there all the time?" Celia said. "Even when I was here?"

"It must have been. Then I went down to get something out of the freezer and there it was."

She was making light of it now. "Alec said it was terrified. That's why it attacked me. He said it was more terrified of me than I was of it."

"What do you think?"

"No way," Rachel said. "You've never seen anybody more terrified than me."

There was a pause, then Celia said, "I'd better tell you why I came."

"I thought it was to see me—or Alec."

"Of course it was, but there's something else. I've lost the ring."

"Ring?"

"The one I bought yesterday, made of Mexican silver. You remember, the woman packed up the handbag and the ring and put them in my shopping bag." Rachel nodded. "Well, when I got home last night I unpacked the shopping bag and there was only the purse. I wondered if you had seen the ring."

"No, I haven't. It may be in my car, of course."

"Could we look?"

They searched, but found nothing.

"Let's see, we got into the car at Chichester Station," Rachel said.

"*Your* car."

"We came back and Penny took my stuff inside . . ."

"I asked her to put my shopping bag into my car."

"Yes, I heard you. And you've looked there?"

"I had the seats out, even had the carpets up."

"Let's have a look on the drive."

They searched the area where the cars had been parked and around the base of the steps, and then Rachel said, "I wonder if it got mixed up with my packages."

She went to the trash can in the kitchen and pulled out tissue paper asd crumpled shopping bags and they went through them.

"You don't think Penny might have seen it and thought it was yours?" Celia said.

"I'll ask her."

Penny had seen nothing. She stood at the kitchen door, frowning in concentration.

"I didn't see nothing like it," she said. "And I would have remembered. I love rings like that."

"You remember putting the shopping bag into my car?" Celia said.

"You were bringing all the parcels into the house," Rachel said. "Mrs. James said, 'That bag's mine,' or something like that. 'Will you put it in my car.'"

"I'm not sure I remember exactly."

"You put my packages in the house and you took Mrs. James's shopping bag and put it in her car. But we've searched in all the wrapping paper and we've looked in the cars and outside. Will you have a look around upstairs? It might have caught in your clothing or . . ."

"I'll look everywhere," Penny said anxiously, and went upstairs.

Celia stepped away from the kitchen table and as she did so she backed into a Dutch dresser that Rachel used as a display for pieces of china of which she was particularly fond. Trying to regain her balance Celia put out a hand and knocked over a tall, slender Royal Copenhagen vase with a pattern of roses on it. She tried to grab it, but it fell to the quarry-tiled floor and smashed.

"What a stupid thing to do!" she said. "Rachel, I'm terribly sorry."

She knelt and began to pick up the pieces as Rachel said, "Don't be silly. It wasn't much of a vase anyway."

Suddenly she heard an exclamation.

"What's that?" Celia said sharply.

Something was glittering near the foot of the dresser and Rachel bent to pick it up. "Look!" she whispered, "it's your ring!"

They stared at each other and Celia took the ring. "It's mine, all right. But how did it get there?"

Rachel shook her head. "God knows. Could it possibly have been in the vase? But how on earth . . . ?"

Celia's eyes flicked upwards to where they could hear Penny moving about.

"You surely don't think . . . ?" Rachel began.

"What else is there to think?"

"That she stole it?"

"It's no use asking me. How do I know what happened? Why

don't you get her down and ask her." There was a stiffness in her tone that Rachel had not heard before.

"I couldn't! I mean . . ."

"Why on earth not?"

"There must be some mistake."

"I'd be fascinated to know how a ring that was wrapped up in a box unwrapped itself and placed itself in a vase on the dresser."

"I'll get Penny down."

But Penny did not know either. She stood like a large, gawky schoolgirl called up before the headmistress, asked to explain something she did not understand. "But you might have forgotten," Rachel said. "You might have unwrapped it just to look at it and then . . ."

"I'm sure I didn't. I *know* I didn't."

"It might have fallen, and you picked it up and put it in there for safekeeping."

"And then it unwrapped itself," Celia said.

"I swear, Mrs. Chater . . ." Penny began, then an expression of horror dawned on her face. "You don't mean you think I took it for myself?"

"Didn't you?" Celia said.

"Of course not," Rachel said, embarrassed.

Penny began to cry. It was like a faucet turned on. Tears cascaded down her cheeks. "I never . . ." she said. "I never done anything like that!"

There were footsteps outside the kitchen and Alec appeared. "Celia! Hello, there . . . what on earth's the matter, Penny?"

Penny, in her distress, failed even to acknowledge him. He put his arm around her shoulders and said gently, "What is it?"

She put both hands up to her face. Mucus was streaming from her nose and she sniffed loudly.

"Celia lost a ring. I found it in that vase," Rachel said.

"And?"

Rachel said nothing.

"And you think Penny took it?" Alec swung his good eye on Celia.

Celia shrugged.

Looking at her, Alec hesitated, then seemed to make up his mind. "I've known Penny's family for years and Penny since she was a baby and nothing like this has ever happened," he said. "Someone has made a mistake."

There was nothing friendly in the cold stare Celia turned on him. For a moment there was silence as he met her eyes steadily. Then she moved toward the door.

"Celia, don't go!" Rachel said.

"Thank you for the coffee."

As she opened the door of her car she turned and said politely, "Perhaps you'd let me know when you get things sorted out." Rachel watched her drive away, feeling sick.

In the house Alec was saying, "Now come on, Penny, a grown girl like you doesn't act like this. Here, take my handkerchief, it's a nice big one." He looked over her shoulder at Rachel. "Now, wipe your eyes and wash your face and have a good blow. Make you feel a lot better. Then, when you feel up to it, come back."

Penny turned away and went toward the downstairs bathroom.

"I'm afraid she's taken it badly," Alec said.

"I know, and I'm terribly sorry. Celia was upset and I suppose she couldn't think of any other explanation. I'm sure there's some mistake. But how *did* it get there?"

"It wasn't Penny," he said flatly. "I've known the family for years and they're as honest as the day is long. Anyway, that's not the only problem now. She says you've accused her of stealing and she can't stay."

"I haven't accused her of anything!"

"She thinks you have."

"Alec, I don't want her to leave! Look, I'll go up to Sophie now. You talk to her. Tell her we need her. Tell her Sophie needs her. Tell her anything you like so long as she stays."

"Lord, what a mess! Well, I'll see what I can do, and then I'd better go to the cottage and soothe Celia down. I didn't mean to make her angry."

He looked suddenly wretched and she wondered if this was the first disagreement he'd had with Celia.

It was half an hour before he emerged from the kitchen. She

had been with Sophie much of the time, then she had stood at the top of the stairs and listened to the rumble of his voice. When he came out, he nodded. Penny would stay.

That afternoon, Celia telephoned. Rachel took the call in Bill's study.

"Rachel, I've called to apologize for this morning. It was one of those stupid things. I got angry and I'm afraid my anger spilled over."

"Penny was pretty upset."

"I know. Now look, I've some other news, which might make you feel better. As I drove out of your gates on the way home I saw a dead cat lying in the grass."

"*My* cat?" She caught herself. She was doing it too.

"It was certainly black. I expect it was knocked over by a car." Relief flooded through her.

"That's something positive, at any rate," Celia went on. "Especially as I've been responsible for you losing Penny."

"Losing her? Didn't Alec tell you? He persuaded her to stay."

"I haven't seen Alec."

"But he was going to see you when he left here, to explain."

"I was out for a while. I must have missed him. You're going to *keep* her?"

"Celia, I'm sure she didn't take your ring."

"You said that this morning. Perhaps you'll explain how you think it happened."

"Maybe it fell out of the box . . ."

"And into a vase? Without either of us noticing?"

"No. But Penny might have picked it up for safekeeping, not knowing whose it was. And then she forgot. Or under pressure panicked and denied everything. It's possible. Anyway, she was so distressed she wanted to leave, but Alec managed to talk her into staying."

"I see." There was a chill in her voice.

"It wasn't easy. She was determined to go. But he has known the family for a long time."

"Yes. Of course, he could talk Penny into anything."

"What do you mean?"

"Nothing. Just don't take too much notice of Alec when he tells you how admirable Penny and her family are."

"I don't understand . . ."

"Forget it, Rachel! You seem to have an impression that Alec's the white knight, that's all. I can tell you, he isn't."

"Celia, I thought you and Alec . . ."

"Well, think again! And if I were you I'd also think very hard about keeping that girl in your house."

When she had hung up the telephone Rachel put on her sheepskin coat and went to the front door. She was frowning. What on earth had Celia been hinting at? There was no doubt she had been hinting at something—but what? Oh God, she thought despairingly, this is never-ending! The mysteries were piling up. Nothing, apparently, was as it seemed. Now she was not to trust Alec . . .

As she opened the door she saw him hurrying up the drive toward her, a shotgun tucked under his arm, square, solid, reliable. Or was he?

"Rachel!" he called. "I've just seen . . ."

"I know," she said. "Celia just telephoned. You don't have to shoot it after all. It must have been run over." She paused, then frowned. "Funny, though, Celia's the only person who's been here in a car today. It must have happened yesterday."

"No. It's been killed within the last couple of hours," he said. "It wasn't there when I left you this morning."

"But it must have been! Celia saw it—and she left before you."

"Well, it wasn't!" he said flatly. "I couldn't have missed it. It's half on the road, half in the grass on the left. Exactly where I walked. Come and see."

She followed him out the gate and as soon as she had left the drive she saw the black, limp body lying on the tarmac.

"I don't know how you . . ." she began, then stopped. Alec had one, dim eye. Nobody else could have missed it, but *he* could.

He read her thoughts. "I know I don't see too well, Rachel, but I tell you, the cat was not here this morning."

"Oh well, it doesn't matter," she said quickly, wanting to avoid an argument that could only emphasize his increasing blindness. "It's dead."

They had reached the body and, feeling slightly sick, she looked down at it, then drew in her breath sharply.

"Alec, this *isn't* the cat!"

"What do you mean?"

"This isn't *my* cat! Look, it's not much more than a kitten. Mine is huge."

He knelt on the road. "Animals always look bigger and more sinister in the dark. Haven't seen any other cats around here, have you?"

"No. But this isn't it. Look at its paws. Is there any injury?"

He examined it. "No. Nothing wrong with any of the legs. Funny, though . . ."

"What?"

He was running his hands over its head, probing in the neck fur.

"What is it?" she said again.

"What . . . ? Oh, nothing. Rachel, could you fetch me a plastic bag or something? I'll get rid of it for you."

When she returned with a green Harrod's shopping bag he bundled the body in and tucked the shotgun under his arm.

"Glad I won't need this," he said. "I'm sure this is your cat. Everything will be all right now, you'll see. No more frights."

But as she watched him stump off toward his cottage she knew in her heart that he was wrong.

That night she was making her usual rounds just after dark, locking up, and was drawing the sitting-room curtains when she heard a scratching on the glass, like fingernails. Her heart almost stopped. She stood, clutching the fabric. Everything was silent. Then it came again. A sort of tapping . . .

She felt the scream in her throat but managed to control it. A modicum of sanity returned and she knew she had to see what was out there. It must be a branch, blown by the dark wind; a thread of the old clematis, now skeleton-like without its leaves. It was, perhaps, nothing more than imagination. But another series of taps, more insistent, were real, and she twitched aside the curtains. Pressed against the glass was the grotesque, animal face she had seen in her dreams: black, triangular, with shining, green pinpoints of light for eyes, a pink mouth open in a silent snarl. One moment it was there, framed by the window and then, abruptly, it was gone and the frame was empty.

13

Alec and Rachel sat side by side on two chairs in the cellar, facing the mesh-covered window. It had been snowing on and off during the afternoon and was very cold.

Alec was on the right, the shotgun on his lap. Rachel held a powerful flashlight. It had not occurred to her that she would have a part in his plan to kill the cat, but when she had called him, hysterically, the previous evening, he had explained that she would have to be his eyes. It was only later she had realized that he had made no further attempt to argue that *her* cat was dead.

Before they took up their positions he had explained his plan. "We'll only have a few seconds. It will come to the window and stop. Then anything can happen. It could get our smell—although the whole cellar must smell of humans—and it'll be gone like a flash. Or else it will be so intent on getting to the food that it will jump through the tear in the mesh into the cellar. I must shoot it in the second when it's framed in the window. Can't try to kill it in here. It's too dangerous in a confined space."

She could feel herself trembling and knew she would have difficulty controlling the light. She could just make out the shape of the plate they had set on the chute, containing the contents of a tin of cat food.

Alec whispered, "Don't forget, I'll have to shoot along the light beam, so you must aim it at the tear in the mesh. Only way I can see with this bloody eye."

They waited in the dark. Once the boiler started up and once the freezer switched itself on. Those were the only noises. They seemed isolated, bound to each other in this, the oldest part of the house. There was something primeval about the situation and about the house itself, crouching at the edge of the Great Forest.

And then the telephone rang. She started to her feet and looked at her watch. It was showing nearly midnight.

She ran up the stairs and felt her knee protest. Having Alec in the house made the insistent ringing less ominous—but this time it *must* be Bill. It was morning in California.

In his study she said, "Hullo?"

There was no reply.

"Hullo?"

Then she heard a ticking as though someone was holding the receiver near a clock. Tick . . . tick . . . tick . . . tick. And silence as the line went dead.

Her knuckles showed white where she was gripping the receiver. Slowly she replaced it in its cradle.

She switched off the study light and as she did so, realized she had forgotten to close the curtains. Snow brightened the darkness outside. The study windows looked over the garden. About an inch of snow had fallen, covering trees and bushes, obliterating the lawn and drive. There was not a mark on it, it was pristine. Out of the corner of her eyes she saw a movement. A black shape was crossing the snow. It stopped by the rhododendron bush. She stared at it for a few seconds, hardly daring to breathe, and then she ran back to the head of the cellar steps.

"Alec!" she hissed. "The cat's in the garden."

She heard his chair scrape back and then he bumped into something which fell with a clatter.

"Sorry about that," he whispered as he came up the steps. "Where is it?"

"I'll show you. You can see it through Bill's window." They crept into the study. "Over by the bushes. It's in the shadow."

"I can't see a thing. Have you got the flashlight?"

"Here."

"Open the window."

"I can't. It's got a burglarproof lock."

They went to the front door and she opened it as silently as she could. There was a click as Alec moved the safety-catch on the gun. "Come close to me," he said. "Remember I have to shoot along the light beam."

Her hands were shaking.

"Now!"

She switched on the flashlight and he fired a second later. The noise in her ears was enormous and there was a harsh smell of cordite. She played the powerful beam on the base of the bush, but could see nothing.

"Are you sure it was there?"

"It was when I called you."

"It may have heard me in the cellar. I'll go out and take a look anyway."

She watched him out in the snow kneeling by the bush, moving the torch backwards and forwards. He came back nearly frozen. "It was there all right. You can see its tracks coming over the snow, but it may have gone by the time I fired."

"What do we do now?"

"We can't do much more tonight. Not after the noise we've made."

The cat had been watching the house from the shadow of the rhododendron bush when it had heard the noise of Alec knocking over Rachel's chair in the cellar, which had sent it into the very heart of the bush itself. When Alec had fired, the pellets had spattered harmlessly over the snowy lawn.

The past week had seen a deterioration in the animal. The infection had extended up its leg, withering the big thigh muscle and entering its body. The leg had stiffened and could not be held clear of the ground, so now, wherever it went, the leg dragged behind. Had Alec's eyes been better, he might have seen the little furrow drawn through the snow by the useless paw.

The cat was very thin and had lost several pounds. Its hipbones stuck out like knuckles and its flanks were hollow. Its face seemed to have narrowed to a thin, fox-like jaw, big staring eyes, and cheeks that had sunk onto the teeth.

It lived precariously, its food supply coming more by good

luck than its own design. As winter closed its fist on the land, and squirrels and rabbits went to their holes and warrens, the carnage on the roads came to a halt and the cat was unable to find carrion. Perforce it had to live closer to humans. So it had given up the den—in any case, it was water-logged—and had taken up residence under the rhododendron bush. The house nearest the Chaters', a small cottage, was owned by a London couple who came down only at weekends. At these times there would be scraps of food and perhaps the good fortune of a garbage can knocked over by scavenging dogs.

During one of the storms of the past ten days two telephone linesmen had come out to repair a flooded junction box.

They had brought their sandwiches and had sat in the yellow van eating their midday meal. But one of the linesmen had had a heavy night and was hung over; he had no stomach for dried-out bread and scraps of ham and cheese. So he had thrown the packet of sandwiches into the nearest hedgerow. The cat had found them. That had been the first good meal it had had for fours days.

Then the snow had come. It had fallen off and on for several days, the skies clearing at night and a hard frost setting in. This had meant that the bird population had difficulty in finding food and, as usual in bitter winter weather, the sparrows and robins attacked the early-morning milk bottles standing on doorsteps. They would peck the foil tops to try and get at the milk. This helped the cat. It smelled the milk and on one doorstep tried to lick it from the holes made by the birds. In doing so, it knocked the bottle over. It smashed and the cat was able to lap up the entire pint.

There was a terrible irony about its life now: to find enough food to maintain life, it had to be in constant motion, searching for carrion, for discarded rubbish; but movement weakened it and drove the poison of the infection farther and farther into its viscera and it moved in a cocoon of pain.

The one place it had found where it had been dry and warm and where there had been a stock of food that it could have without great effort had been the Chaters' cellar. It was waiting for its chance to return.

        ❊   ❊   ❊

Rachel was dreaming. Anyone standing in the bedroom watching her would have seen her body twisting and her eyelids fluttering, her hands clenching and unclenching. She moved from side to side and sometimes her body would jerk as though her dream had startled her. A faint dew of sweat stood on her forehead.

She woke, suddenly and harshly, shuddering with fright. Sunlight was streaming into the bedroom in huge, square blocks of orange. She thought for a moment that she was in Santa Monica. She thought she could hear the sea. For a brief second she wondered whether Michael had left for the studios. Then the present reasserted itself. She was in her own room, it was a winter's morning, and Bill was away. She knew she had been dreaming, but she could not remember the dream. It stayed with her as an aftertaste, a feeling of unease, of things that had not been made known to her: miasmic horrors, creatures from the canvases of Hieronymus Bosch.

She lay fighting its aftereffects until her mind took her into other channels and she recalled the night before: Alec in the cellar, the shotgun's blast through the front door, the telephone ringing, and the ticking. She looked at her watch; it was almost noon. She had slept badly during the night, even though Alec had stayed in the spare room. She had taken him back to his own cottage on her way to fetch Penny, had come back exhausted, returned to bed, and fallen asleep.

The day had been misty early on but now it was a blazing clear winter's day. She looked out of the window. It was like magic. The snow had gone, the trees were brown, the grass was green, the sun shone, and when she opened the window she felt a mild breeze from the south. It was more like an early autumn day. Everything was shining with melted water.

She went into Sophie's room. The crib was empty.

"Penny!" she shouted. "Penny!" She ran to the stairs.

Penny appeared from the kitchen.

"Where's Sophie?"

"I thought you'd gone out. I thought I heard the car."

"Where's Sophie?"

Rachel went down the stairs, ignoring the jarring of her knee.

123

"She's outside," Penny said. "It's such a lovely day. I put her in her carriage."

She should have felt a flood of relief but the dream had left her mind defenseless. "Where did you put her?"

"Out by the lily pond."

Ever since Rachel had seen *Sunset Boulevard* and William Holden's body hanging suspended in a swimming pool she had nursed a secret dread that one day she would look out of a window and see the same thing. She felt the terror rush in on her: was it to be Sophie's body?

She flung open the side door and went out onto the paved terrace in the corner made by the *L* shape of the house. The pond sparkled in the sunshine, making arabesques of golden light on the side of the house. The only things in the water were a few dead leaves. With a feeling of relief she went forward to the carriage. She could not see Sophie's head. The child was almost invisible. The pillow was over her face. Rachel wrenched it off. Sophie's little face had a bluish tinge.

All the fears she had ever had as a mother crystallized in that one moment. For a second she stood rigid, then she grabbed the baby and ran into the house, shouting at Penny to phone the doctor. She put Sophie down on the kitchen table and unzipped her jumpsuit. She could feel a faint fluttering of the heart, but the small body did not seem to be breathing. She had seen pictures of what to do in such a case, but she had never paid much attention to them. All she knew was that she should put her lips on the victim's mouth and breathe. She put her mouth over Sophie's and breathed in and out, trying to force air into her lungs, being one with her like a breathing-machine acting for them both. She heard Penny at the telephone and heard her return.

"The doctor's having his surgery. Do you want to speak to him?" Penny said.

She shook her head, frightened to take her mouth from Sophie's. She went on sucking and blowing until finally there was a response. She felt breath come into her own mouth and when she pulled away and looked down the blue tinge was disappearing and the flesh of Sophie's face was turning to its normal pink. She gathered her up and ran to the car.

* * *

"But how could it have happened?" She was sitting in Dr. Williams's office and Sophie was on her knee.

He played with his half-lens glasses, then settled them on his nose. "This is your first child, isn't it, Mrs. Chater? I think what happened should tell you something." He scratched his short, gray-black hair. "*Anything* can happen where babies are concerned."

Sophie reached for a ballpoint pen that was lying on his desk. Automatically, Rachel moved it.

"I've read about crib deaths," she said.

He shook his head. "Whatever you've read, believe me, what happened—or what nearly happened—to your baby has nothing to do with what we know as a cot death. We still don't know much about them, but we think they are probably caused by massive viral infections. Your baby somehow got her pillow over her face and nearly smothered."

"That's what I don't understand. I just don't understand how she could."

"She's all right now, anyway. I'd let her do without a pillow for a while if I were you."

"I'll make sure of it—and she won't be out of my sight."

"I don't recommend that. Babies have to take their chance in life like everyone else. Treat her normally. Don't let this get you down or you may have worse trouble."

It was when she was giving Sophie her bottle an hour later that she noticed the scratch on her neck.

It was not a big scratch and it was hidden by a fold of skin, only becoming visible when the baby turned her head away from the bottle. Rachel stretched the skin between her fingers. She stared at the red line and another scratch came before her inner eye: the one on Franco's muzzle, through which he had bled to death. She bit her lip until she winced with pain. Stop it, she said to herself, stop it! The scratch could have been made in any of a dozen ways.

When she had finished feeding Sophie she went to look at the carriage. She picked up the offending pillow. Underneath it were some crumbs and a single black hair. And then, on the side of the pram, she saw marks that looked as though they might have been made with a knife.

Alec came around the corner of the house. "Isn't it a lovely day?" he said. "We sometimes get 'em in an English winter. Makes up for all the rest."

"Alec, I want you to see something," she said, as calmly as she could.

"Seeing isn't exactly my strong suit," he said, smiling.

Even in her preoccupation she noticed that he was looking pale and tired; the patchwork marks on his face were more obvious than usual. But she had no inclination, at the moment, to waste time worrying about Alec.

"What do these look like?" She pointed to the marks on the carriage.

"Scratches." He touched them with the tips of his fingers.

"And what's that?"

"A black hair."

"I want you to come with me."

She took him upstairs to Sophie's room. The baby was lying on her back, gurgling.

Alec gave her his finger. "My word, you've got a grip!"

Rachel pulled down the zip of the child's jumpsuit and revealed the scratch. "What about that?"

"It's a scratch."

"Yes. Come and have a drink."

"It's a little early, isn't it?"

"I need one."

"All right. I'll have a beer."

She gave him one and poured a whiskey for herself. "Sit down. I want to tell you something."

She described what had happened that morning, from the time she awoke to the time she had seen Sophie almost dead in her carriage, to the struggle she'd had bringing life back into the child, to her visit to the doctor.

"Good God, what a dreadful thing to have happened!" he said. "I see why you need the drink."

"That's not the whole reason."

"No?"

"Haven't you put it together?"

"Put what together?"

"The scratches. There were scratches on the carriage. A scratch on Sophie's neck."

"Christ! You don't believe—?"

"Why not?"

"You've become obsessed by that damned cat! If the house burned down you'd say you saw it running around with matches."

"That's not very funny."

"It's not meant to be. One minute you're accusing the cat of luring a dog up to a farm and feeding it on Warfarin, then scratching it, which, apart from anything else, implies that the cat knew that Warfarin is an anticoagulant. I mean, I've never heard anything so preposterous in my life. Now you accuse it of an attempt to murder Sophie. That's what it boils down to. What you're saying is that it jumped up into the carriage, put the pillow over her face, and in doing so scratched her on the neck. Good God, Rachel!"

As they stared at each other, Penny came into the room. "The soap powder's run out," she said.

"I'll get some later," Rachel said. "Penny, when you put Sophie down this morning, did you notice any scratches on the side of the pram?"

"No."

"Oh, so *you* put her down?" Alec said.

"Yes."

"You didn't see the cat anywhere around, did you?"

"What cat?"

"The one that's gone wild. The one that upset your garbage can."

"No. I just put her out there and give her a cracker and . . ."

"You what?" Rachel said.

"I give her a cracker." Anxiety crossed her face at the thought that she might have done something wrong.

"And you left her eating the cracker?"

"Yes."

When she had gone Alec said, "Have I got it right? Penny put her down and gave her a cracker?"

"That's what she said."

"Well, now, the cat may have gone after that, I grant you. If it was starving or as hungry as we think, it might have taken the cracker away from Sophie. Those *could* be its claw marks on the carriage. And the scratch on her neck just *might* have been made at the same time. But all this is a long shot. I mean, I'm being the devil's advocate. The cat *might* have jumped up; *might* have taken her cracker; *might* have scratched her in doing so. But the cat certainly didn't put a pillow over her face."

There was a long moment of silence as the words penetrated her consciousness.

Even her obsessive horror of the animal could not deny their truth. But if she was right, and Alec was right, what *had* caused the pillow to move from under Sophie's head and nearly smother her?

14

Her dream took a different turn after that. Gone was the face at the window, the trickle of blood, the car slithering off the road; now it was always the cat, the dark, furry shape. Sometimes she saw it stalking the carriage, sometimes scrabbling up the side, its back legs seeking purchase, sometimes crouching over Sophie.

Rachel would wake, shuddering, and hurry out of bed to the baby's crib. Despite the doctor's warning, she carried Sophie wherever she went in the house, left her only when Penny promised not to take her eyes off her. She no longer left her outside in her carriage and at night she moved the crib into her own room.

She and Alec kept vigil in the cellar for two consecutive nights, but their presence must have signaled itself in scent or noises, for the cat did not come.

Before she drove him home on the third morning, he said, "This is hopeless, Rachel. It won't come while we're sitting down there. I've had an idea. With your permission, I'm going to fix a booby trap."

"Anything, if you think it will work."

First he borrowed two wood clamps from Bill's workshop and clamped the gun to a beam, its barrel pointing at the hole in the wire mesh on the window. Then he found a ball of thin kitchen string and covered a length of it in black shoe polish.

"We used to do this in North Africa whenever we overran a village where there had been Eyeties or Jerries," he said. "Once I fixed one like this in a villa in Libya. The Jerries had evacuated it, but we knew they'd come back as soon as we left. Not through the door, they'd be too suspicious to do that. So I set the gun up to cover one of the windows. Any clever chap who thought he'd avoid the door got his head blown off when he climbed in through the window."

He talked with boyish enthusiasm as he worked, the fascination of the booby trap outweighing any scruples he might have had about assassinating what was, to him, a harmless animal. Rachel watched as he tapped in several staples along the beam and window frame. He fixed one end of the string to the window and ran it across the hole. Then he threaded it through the staples on the beam and looped it around the trigger of the shotgun.

"See? Any pressure on the string pulls the trigger," he said. "And the cat can't avoid the string when it comes through the window."

He went outside to the window, crouched down, and said, "I'm the cat. Now watch." He put his hand through the mesh, touching the black string. He pushed and there was a click as the gun fired on an empty breech. "Right," he said. "When it gets dark I'll put in the cartridge."

But the cat did not appear that night, nor the following one. Alec arrived each afternoon at about half past four, as darkness fell. He would check the gun, she would give him tea, and he would return to his cottage.

Apart from this, her life became like the cat's, almost totally isolated, for she saw nothing even of Celia, who, when she called her once, sounded aloof and unwelcoming; Rachel realized that she must still be annoyed about the incident involving Penny and her ring.

She noticed that Alec, too, had become more taciturn and often seemed preoccupied. The former ease appeared to have gone from their relationship. She did not even know whether he had patched up matters with Celia and did not like to ask.

She seemed always to be waiting: waiting for the dark, waiting for something to happen. She had letters from Bill and she wrote to him, but in the background as she wrote now was the specter of Sally. Had they met? Could she, even, be with him in the cabin, leaning over his shoulder as he read his letters, laughing quietly at the way they were fooling Rachel? Her letters became briefer, stilted. She wrote about Sophie and Penny and Alec, but she did not mention the cat or her fears. Almost unconsciously, she was determined not to reveal herself to him—to *them*.

His communications, too, were short, though apparently warm and loving, and in one he protested about her lack of news. He wrote, "Darling, I can't believe you have nothing more to tell me than that Sophie is well, that it is cold, that Penny dusted the decanters this morning without being asked. Can't you understand that I want to know about *you*? It's only the knowing that keeps me from going crazy out here. For instance, you said you were going to London with some woman you met at the Renshaws. Tell me about London, and what you bought and where you went and how you felt. *Everything!*"

So she devoted an entire letter to London and, as she wrote, some of the inhibitions faded and she could almost feel she was talking to him, that nothing had changed. The next morning she went to the mailbox a few hundred yards down the lane. It was a lovely day and, for once, she allowed herself to think about him: not about Sally's husband, but about the Bill she knew. By the time she reached the house again, she was almost desperate with longing for him and, as she passed his garden workroom, she remembered that at least there was a way she could hear his voice. His tapes must be there somewhere, because he had said before he left that some of the dictation had already been typed and he would be taking the manuscript with him to America. She looked on his shelves, then went through the desk drawers, but there were no cassettes, and eventually she decided that he had probably taken them with him to reuse. But simply being in his room gave her comfort and she wandered about it, touching the things he had touched, remembering how he had looked.

And then, as she sat at his typewriter and slid her fingers over the keys, she noticed a sheet of paper almost hidden under the thick felt cushion on which the machine stood. She pulled it out. It was a creased sheet of the legal paper he used for his first drafts, and there was typing on it. Her eyes moved down the page and she began to tremble uncontrollably. She was reading her dream.

"The tapping at the window . . . the man's face with blood pouring from a wound . . . dark holes for eyes . . . the wife screams, because she sees the cat . . ."

The notes became even scrappier: "The story is about a woman who has car crash and kills . . . *not* kills: *someone* is killed. Not her fault. She filled with guilt . . . has dreams. An easy victim. Her husband having it off with another woman . . . Husband and other woman decide to drive wife insane. Why . . . ?" There was a scratching out here as though he had had an idea and then dropped it. "No . . . better still: they hope she will push herself over the edge. Kill herself. Is this believable? Don't know. There was a case like this which Spilsbury handled . . . look it up. Husband and mistress . . ."

The stream of consciousness ended abruptly. There was a series of blank lines, then at the bottom of the page he had scribbled, "Setting: California coast around San Simeon and Carmel."

That was all. As she stared at the page, the words blurred: this was her story. She was the wife and the reference was to her accident. But what was the talk of another woman and attempts to drive the wife insane? Oh God, she thought, Bill and Sally. Her mind flew back to the days when she had been in the hospital: he could have been seeing Sally then. They could have arranged to meet in America. And were planning to drive her, the unwanted second wife, to the point of insanity so they could be together again.

At this point, something seemed to explode in her mind and commonsense burst through her horror. *You stupid bitch!* she heard herself saying into the silence of the little room. People don't *do* such things! This is a page of notes for Bill's new book. Then she thought, But how had he known about the dream? She was sure she had not told him about it when she got home. And she had not told him in the hospital. Or had she? Think. She tried to re-create the environment. The small hospital room took shape in her mind: the window, the chair, the bed. Someone was in the bed—herself—and someone was sitting in the chair—Bill. She was coming out of the anesthetic. She was talking, mumbling. She was crying. Why? Because of the dream. It had first come to her when she was under the anesthetic. She remembered now. She had dreamed of the cat, of the face at the window. That's why she had been crying. She had been frightened. And she had woken to find Bill beside her. The relief had been tremendous. He had comforted her, and she had told him about the dream.

So he had used it as an idea for the novel. But that still left the lovers to explain. She remembered that he had refused to tell her the plot, using the excuse that he wanted her to read the finished manuscript.

Clutching the piece of paper, she went back into the house. Penny was upstairs with Sophie. She could hear the baby gurgling, and Penny's giggle.

In the sitting room, she lit a cigarette and, as she had done after the accident, she began, deliberately, to go over everything that had happened since she arrived home. It was as though the shock of her discovery had cleared away a mist in which she seemed to have been moving during the past weeks.

Put it together, she told herself. Recognize that something has been happening here that can be explained. You are a rational woman, and yet you live in constant fear. Think it out . . .

She had come home from the hospital and Bill, almost immediately, had left for California. Then she had learned about Sally, the first wife of whom he never spoke but who had, according to Celia, been very much in love with him. He had not even mentioned the child they had had. Why? And Sally had gone to Hollywood.

The cat: was it her own guilt after the accident that made her exaggerate the part the cat was playing? But it *had* attacked her in the cellar and it had been watching her through the window. Wait: in each case, hadn't the cat been behaving normally? In the cellar it had been frightened, as Alec said, and had been trying to escape. The window: cats often sat on sills and peered into rooms. She had assumed it had scratched Sophie, but the scratches had not necessarily been made by a cat's claws. And yet, what human being would be vicious enough to hurt a sleeping baby? The cat . . .

Leave that for a moment. Guilty or not, the mere thought of the black, triangular face and the brilliant eyes made her shudder.

There had been the words added to her "Welcome home," the

smashed cherub, the mysterious telephone calls. The pillow over Sophie's face.

It was at that moment that she became convinced that she was being deliberately terrorized, not only by the cat—it became suddenly less important—but by a human enemy as well. But who? And why?

Her mind, trained as Bill's was to the development of ideas, began to race. What if, in seeking a plot for his novel, he had given her the clue? Its inspiration had been her accident. A woman and a man are in a car. They crash and the man is killed. But instead of Bill's thesis, suppose the dead man's wife thinks he has been having an affair with the woman who drove the car, and she wants revenge? Revenge was a common enough motive. Prisons all over the world were filled with people who had taken revenge on their mothers, on their fathers, their sisters, brothers, on society. She could imagine such a dark emotion flourishing in Lexton, for it was part of the tradition of the Great Forest, of the ancient tribe of the South Saxons. She had attributed the revenge motive to the cat, but suppose a human being also sought revenge on her?

The memory of Sophie's face covered by the pillow returned to her. She felt the surface of her skin crawl as she began to rewind the tape of her mind to that day. It had been the morning after the first abortive attempt to kill the cat. She had seen the animal in the snow. Alec had fired and hit nothing. Then he had gone to bed and she had gone to bed, though not to sleep. She had taken him home in the morning, had fetched Penny, and then felt so tired she had lain down and fallen asleep almost immediately. She had wakened sweating and shaking from dreams that eluded memory. She remembered the blocks of orange sunshine on the bedroom carpet. She had gone into Sophie's room and seen the empty crib. The legacy of the dreams had made her terrified that something had happened. She had shouted for Penny. She remembered her relief when Penny told her she had put Sophie outside because it was such a lovely day. But relief had turned to horror as she found her baby more dead than alive.

Stop.

She stopped the memory tape, for this was where detail was vital and she needed Penny.

She ran upstairs. Penny was sitting crosslegged on the carpet, tickling Sophie, whose legs and arms were waving like flowers in a high wind.

"Penny, can you remember the morning when Sophie had her . . . her accident?" Rachel said.

The picture was clear in her own mind, but she wanted Penny to confirm it: Sophie had been lying on her back, her arms tucked in, the blankets tucked tightly under the mattress. It was the blankets that had held her immobile so she had been unable to fight off the smothering pillow.

"Of course I can, Mrs. Chater."

"Something has occurred to me. Tell me again exactly what happened."

"Well, you was asleep and Sophie started to cry," Penny said. "Not for devilment, but for company, like. So I changed her and brought her down and I played with her in the kitchen for a little while, but I had my work. So seeing as it was such a lovely day I took her outside and put her in her carriage and give her a cracker—"

"Stop there," Rachel said. "You gave her a cracker?"

The anxious look came over Penny's large, doughy face again. "Yes . . ."

"It's all right. I don't mind. They're good for her teeth. What I'm getting at is, you didn't tuck her in, did you?"

Penny looked puzzled. "I couldn't tuck her in with a cracker in her hands," she said finally.

There it was, Rachel thought, the indisputable fact. Sophie could not have eaten a cracker if her arms were tucked under the blankets and she could not have tucked herself in because she was a tiny baby, and if Penny hadn't tucked her in and Rachel hadn't tucked her in . . .

". . . heard you call from the stairs," Penny was saying, continuing her account because Rachel had not told her to stop. "And I remember thinking, Funny, I thought I'd heard you go out. I thought I heard the car."

"And then I went out and found Sophie," Rachel said.

Her thoughts were chaotic but they always returned to the

same point: who had tucked Sophie in and then placed a pillow over her face? It was conceivable—just—that a cat—*the* cat—might have jumped into the carriage and scratched the child, but no cat had carefully arranged the blankets and the pillow in a deliberate attempt to murder Sophie.

Rachel suddenly saw a vision of her baby as she might have been had she not been found in time: a tiny, lifeless body, a round face that would never smile again. Rage held her for a moment, and when she was relatively calm again she determined that she would find the person who had done it. But first she had to try and think out the situation rationally.

There had to be a reason why someone would do such a thing, and the reason had to be Rachel herself. Someone hated her enough to plan a deliberate campaign to terrorize her and then, in a final attempt to break her, was prepared to kill her baby.

Without even being aware of it, she had returned to the sitting room and was standing, staring out of the window as she thought of the people she knew.

It could not have been Penny. She loved the child. Or was there some dark aspect of her mind that Rachel had not fathomed?

Or Alec? He might have seen Sophie in her carriage and thought she was cold. He might, in all innocence, have tucked her in, but would he put a pillow over her face?

Suddenly she remembered something Celia had said: "You seem to have an impression that Alec's the white knight. I can tell you, he isn't . . ."

She hurried to the telephone. When Celia answered she said, without preliminary, "I have to ask you something. Last time we talked you hinted that there was something wrong with Alec."

"Surely not! I'm fond of Alec."

"You said that I shouldn't take any notice of anything Alec said about Penny and her family. What did you mean?"

"Oh, that!"

"Tell me."

"Well . . ." Celia hesitated. "I only said it because I was worried about Penny stealing your silver, or something."

"*What was it?*"

"Alec's supposed to have had an affair with Penny's mother."

"What? While his wife was alive?"

"Yes. Penny's family kept a couple of horses and he was always round there, allegedly treating them. But it was only an excuse."

"Are you sure?"

"Penny may even be his daughter, for all I know."

"And that's it? I mean, you don't know anything else about him?"

"Only what we all know. What is this all about?"

But Rachel had hung up.

She felt a curious mixture of distaste and relief. The picture of Alec having an affair with Penny's mother was not attractive, but in no way could it suggest a reason for him to murder a baby.

So neither he nor Penny had an obvious motive. Who else?

As soon as the third name came into her mind she realized that it had been there, in the background, all along. Subconsciously, she had been avoiding the moment when she must recognize that there *was* one person with a rational motive for killing Sophie, one person who might want to take revenge on Rachel herself: Mrs. Leech.

She shivered. Now that the name had surfaced, she would have to confront the woman, and who could predict the chain reaction that might set off?

Then she thought again of what might have happened to Sophie, and her resolve hardened. As she drove through the lanes she clung to her anger, and by the time she reached Mrs. Leech's cottage it had settled into a steady, consuming determination to make the woman admit what she had done and take the consequences.

15

Rachel banged angrily on the front door of the Leech cottage and it was opened by the little girl she had seen before. She held a broken doll and her face needed a wash.

"Mum!" she shouted. "Mum, it's that lady!"

Rachel pushed past her and went into the kitchen. Mrs. Leech turned away from the stove, where she was heating a tin of spaghetti.

"What do you want?" she said.

"I want to talk to you."

"I got nothing to say to you."

"I have a lot to say to you and I can't say it in front of your daughter."

The room was in the same filthy condition. The damp above the sink was worse and there was a smell of urine that Rachel had not noticed before. Mrs. Leech hesitated, then said, "Go and read your comic."

"Don't want to."

"You hear me?"

"Don't *want* to!"

"I'll give you such a smack if you don't do what I say!"

The child's eyes began to fill with tears. Normally Rachel would have been touched, but now she stood stiffly, waiting. The little girl ran out of the room, slamming the door behind her.

"Well?" her mother said.

"You tried to kill my baby!"

Mrs. Leech was taken aback as much by the statement as the force with which it was said. Rachel came forward a pace or two and the other woman seemed to think she might be physically attacked, for she retreated until her back was almost against the stove.

"You're mad!" she said.

"You came to my house and you took a pillow and you put it over my baby's face. You tried to smother her."

"You're round the bend! I never done nothing like that. I never heard such rubbish in my life. You get out of my house before I call the police."

She started for the kitchen door but Rachel grabbed her wrist. "If you go to the police I'll tell them that you came to my house and that you tried to smother my child. I'll tell them I saw you! I'll tell them I was looking out of a window and I saw you!"

"You wouldn't!"

"I'll tell them that you did it because you were taking revenge on me for what happened to your husband."

Mrs. Leech jerked her hand away and gathered her courage. "They'd never believe it!"

"Why wouldn't they? You believe I was having an affair with your husband. Why wouldn't they believe it?"

The woman blinked and moved away, putting the kitchen table between them. "I don't know what you're on about. I don't know what you want, but I swear to you I ain't never been near your house except just that twice. I never even seen your baby!"

"So you *have* been to my house!"

The spirit seemed to drain out of Mrs. Leech. It was a physical as well as a mental collapse. Her body shrank. She slumped into a chair, put her elbows on the table, and held her head in her hands.

"I know it was bad," she said. "And I was sorry afterwards. As true as God, I was sorry. I never done nothing like that before. But Charlie . . . he meant everything to me. He was my life. We knew each other since we were five years old. We were always going to get married. We had pretend weddings when we were kids. He never looked at another girl, I never looked at another boy, all the way through school. We was married young. Charlie was eighteen and me just turned sixteen. And then . . ." She paused and when she spoke again Rachel heard total misery in her voice. "And then I started having kids and it was difficult for

Charlie to . . . well, you know . . . so he started having other women." She looked up. "Like you."

"Go on."

"It was when you was coming back from the hospital. I seen that sign up on the gate. I dunno why I did it, something just come over me. You was alive and there was your husband and your house and Charlie was dead and me left with the kids and everything. And so—"

"So you wrote 'you bitch' under it."

She nodded. "I thought you'd just think it was kids."

"You said you came twice."

"It was a day or two after that. I was going past your gate again and I saw the little statue and I thought, You bloody bitch, and I pushed it over and its head came off and, I dunno why, but I picked up the head and I carried it a little way up the lane and threw it in the ditch. And that's all. That's all I ever done to you. I'm sorry for it, but I couldn't help myself."

Rachel stared down at her. There was a ring of truth in what she had said. "You swear to me that you never came to my house again?"

Mrs. Leech leaned toward her and her thin, pallid face was contorted with the strain of her effort to convince. "I swear before God, Mrs. . . . Mrs. Chater," she said. "I never been near your house except that twice."

Curiously, it was the woman's use of her name for the first time, as much as her obvious sincerity, that convinced Rachel she was telling the truth. In her desperate effort to reach across the barrier that separated them she had seized upon the only thing she could think of to use as a bridge: Rachel's name.

Rachel's anger drained away, leaving her limp. After a few seconds she said, "I guess I believe you. And this is true, too: I never had an affair with your husband. I never wanted to have an affair with him." For a brief second her mind visualized the scene in the kitchen, Charlie's hands under her arms, cupping her breasts. "He never touched me," she said. "And I never wanted him to." She turned on her heel and left the cottage.

As she went up the steps of her own house she heard the telephone ringing. "I'll get it," she called. She picked up the receiver. "Hello?"

There was a click and then the muffled voice she had heard once before. She still could not make out words, but there was something about the tone that touched a spring in her. "Stop it!" she shouted. "Stop it! Let me alone!" There was another click and the dial tone. Whose voice had it been? Whose? And then she had a dreadful thought: was it anyone's? Was she hearing the voice at all? Why did she hear it sometimes and not others? Was she slipping—the phrase came back to her from Bill's notes —"over the edge"?

She went into the kitchen and said to Penny, "Have there been any calls in the past few days that you've forgotten to tell me about?"

Penny frowned in concentration. "No . . . only . . ."

"Only?"

"There was one yesterday when you were outside. I answered but there wasn't anyone there. It must have been a wrong number."

When she came back from Addiscombe that evening she took the receiver off the hook and placed it on Bill's desk. Now no one could telephone her. She was isolated. Cut off.

Inevitably, her mind went back to Mrs. Leech. She had believed her story, but what if the woman were simply a consummate actress? What if she had admitted to the two visits to lend veracity to her innocence, thereby enabling her to bury the attack on the child? But was she clever enough? Rachel knew in her own mind that she was not, and she was forced to think again of the possibility of Alec and Penny. Had he, perhaps, come down to see Penny? She recalled how angry he had been when she had been accused of stealing the ring. Had he come to see his *daughter?* Was there some undercurrent between the two of them about which Rachel knew nothing but which, in some inexplicable way, was endangering not only herself but her child as well? Could Alec be making the telephone calls?

Then, almost by accident, as she went over in her mind what Penny had told her, she came across something that did not fit. She tried to recall Penny's exact words: "I thought I'd heard you go out. I thought I heard the car." Had she said "the car" or "a car"? Either way, it ruled out Mrs. Leech, for she had no car, and it ruled out Alec, for he could not see to drive. There was only one person she knew whom it did not rule out.

16

"What I'm doing now is racking the wine off the lees," Alec said. "Lovely phrase, that, don't you think? The wine has finished fermenting and is beginning to clear, so I'm going to siphon it into another jar." The new wine began to run from one glass demijohn to the other.

They were in his kitchen. Rachel was standing at the window, half listening, half brooding on her own thoughts. She had gone to see Alec because he was the only person to whom she felt she could talk. In the light of a bright, frosty winter's day, with the sun turning the snow to silver, her conclusions of the previous evening seemed crazy. But she knew she had to talk to someone. As she walked through the fields, hunched into her sheepskin jacket, treading carefully so as not to wrench her knee, she imagined how she was going to sound. Some mysterious enemy is trying, not only to frighten me out of my mind, but to kill my child. Someone who must know me . . . At that point, she almost turned back, because it occurred to her that vagrants sometimes wandered the lanes of Sussex. She pictured a half-starved tramp slinking up her drive, seeing the baby chewing its cracker. Perhaps he had bent over the carriage, grabbed the piece of dry toast, and, as Sophie had opened her mouth to yell with righteous fury, thrust the pillow over her face to stop the noise and fled. But would he have taken the time to tuck in the blankets? How could he have made the scratches on the carriage and on Sophie's neck? She had gone on steadily toward Alec's cottage.

"I'll leave it for a month or so, and rack it again," he said. "You should try making wine. Give you something to do."

She broke in: "Alec, would you say that I was a rational human being?"

He swung his good eye onto her. "Big question, that," he said, smiling. "I've always wondered about rationalism and women. Pragmatism, yes, but rationalism means logic and—"

"I'm serious, Alec."

"Well, since you ask, I would have to say that I've been doubtful."

"You mean because of the cat?"

"That's exactly what I mean."

"Things have been happening that are difficult to explain. When unexplained things happen, you get confused."

"Of course you do, love, especially after an accident like yours."

She moved away from the window and sat down in a straight chair. "It's not a nice feeling to know that someone hates you."

"Oh, come on now! You're exaggerating again."

"No, it's true. My only problem is how do I convince you. Everything I say you'll put down to exaggeration or imagination. You know how it is when people think someone is—is insane, when they're not; then whatever they do to try and prove their own sanity, the more mad they seem."

Bubbles began to appear in the plastic tube and Alec moved it deeper into the wine.

"What exactly is bothering you?" he said.

This was the point at which she could stop. It had taken courage to go to him, but he was all she had. During her walk she had realized, with a sense of pain, that she was a total stranger in this enclosed English landscape. That without Bill she had almost no individual existence. She was cut off from her roots, from people she had grown up with, worked with, gone to school with. In San Francisco or Los Angeles she would only have had to lift a telephone to be able to communicate with someone who knew her. Here her relationships had been on the most superficial level: going out for drinks with so-and-so, or having so-and-so in for drinks; dining out, returning the invitation. And all the people mere acquaintances.

Alec took off his striped apron and said, "Come through to the sitting room, have a glass of wine, and tell your Uncle Alec." He built up the fire and poured her a glass of rosé.

She told her story without emotion, watching herself, playing the game she had described to him earlier of the same person who needs to convince others of his sanity. Imagination, exaggeration: those were the two words she had used, and she was careful not to color her story. She began on the day she had come out of the hospital. She told him about her return to the house, about the unlikable Nurse Griffin, the writing on the welcome home sign, the headless statue, the telephone calls. She repeated the incidents he already knew concerning the cat and she told them without excitement so that he, by comparing what he knew himself with what she was saying, would be forced to recognize that she was telling the unvarnished truth. She wove Celia and their growing friendship into her story, the association that had its high point on the day they had spent in London.

Keeping the same even tone, she recalled the horror of Sophie's near-death, described her own depression and the fear that her mind was becoming infected, and her visit to Mrs. Leech. Then she told him about Bill's first wife and the notes she had found under his typewriter.

His strange face had been immobile throughout her recollection; now his eyebrows shot up.

"But surely the two—er, situations are separate?" he said. "I mean, what on earth can Bill's first wife have to do with the other incidents? She's in America, you said."

"That's what Celia told me."

"Then she can't have anything to do with the phone calls, nor what happened to Sophie."

"No. I wasn't thinking she had, but I can't help feeling that the whole series of events are connected somehow, and, Alec, there's one person who could be the—the catalyst."

There was a pause; then he said, softly, "You mean Celia?"

She nodded, not daring to look at him, wondering when his anger would break through.

Instead he said, "Why do you think she is doing this to you—if she is?"

She shrugged. "She was Sally's friend. Could she be doing it for Sally? I mean, it would all fit, wouldn't it? The plot in the book. Oh God, Alec, suppose Bill wants to get rid of me and go back to her! Maybe Celia is giving them a helping hand, trying to make me go off my head, or run away and leave Bill, or something."

"Rachel, my dear, do you seriously believe Bill would have anything to do with such an appalling idea? You know him a great deal better than I do, but I can tell you categorically that he would not."

"I'm beginning to wonder if I know him at all. There's so much about himself he has never told me. His child by Sally, for instance."

"He told you how unhappy his marriage had been. Seems to me natural he would want to forget it, especially now he is so contented with you and Sophie. Anyhow, from what you say, it's by no means certain Celia's friend *was* Bill's first wife. No, you've let your imagination run away with you, love. Remember those depressions you had after Sophie was born? You're a writer and writers have vivid imaginations or they wouldn't be writers. I believe that now, after the trauma of the accident, you're having another postoperative gloom, so to speak."

"No, that was different. I grant you I imagined all sorts of nonsense then, but this is real. Alec, I did *not* imagine the telephone calls, or the footsteps. I know that now. Or the pillow over Sophie's face. Or that cat at the window. Could it have been put there, do you think, deliberately, to frighten me?"

"You—you mentioned Celia. Do you have any grounds for thinking her capable of such things, apart from the fact that she knew Sally?"

She offered him a cigarette and as he took it she noticed that his hand was shaking.

"I have a feeling that someone wants to isolate me," she said, avoiding a direct answer. "Franco was poisoned. Then there was the ring incident and Celia was annoyed because I did not sack Penny. If I had, I wouldn't have had anyone in the house. Oh, Alec, I'm sorry! I know it all sounds ridiculous. Sometimes I wonder if I *am* going crazy!"

"Let me give you another glass of wine." He stood up and turned his back on her. "Why have you told *me* all this?"

"There isn't anyone else. I guess that really I wanted you to tell me I should go to the police. But clearly I can't. Not with a story that sounds unlikely even to me, when I tell it. And you don't believe a word of it."

"It isn't a case of believing. Of course I believe some of those things happened. It's a question of emphasis. You see everything subjectively. You're lonely and imaginative. You're in a strange country, with few friends. But everything, Rachel, has a rational explanation."

"Okay, tell me."

"Right. Start with the cat. There are dozens of cats in this area. The one you hit could be dead already. You're seeing others, but you had it fixed firmly in your mind that the *one* animal was deliberately terrorizing you. That's your feeling of guilt, Rachel, nothing more. Charlie's dead so you can't focus it on him and you substitute the cat that was injured in the same accident."

"Go on."

"You've already found your own explanation for the defacing of the sign and the statue. Now, the telephone calls. Alas, the countryside is full of nuts, of one kind or another, the heavy breathers, the obscene callers. Yours is simply a variation on the theme: some chap who's picked your number from the book and is calling to see what kind of a reaction he gets. Sophie's accident: she was eating her cracker, the cat—*a* cat—jumped into the carriage and took it, scratching her neck at the same time. You thought of it yourself, remember!"

"And tucked her in so her arms were tight by her sides? And drove away in a car?"

"Who told you all that? Penny, wasn't it? I'm fond of Penny and her family but, let's face it, though the child is the kindest creature in the world, she is inclined to be slow and her memory is unreliable."

She was suddenly tired of Alec; tired of his wine and his stories and his avuncular manner; tired of his patched face and his bravery, his sweet reasonableness. So he thought he had explained everything away. But the incidents had not happened to him. He hadn't listened to the weird telephone voice, the silences, or seen Sophie's blue face, or felt the eyes watching in the garden and the fields.

She stood up abruptly and, almost without farewell, left him.

She did not even glance in the window as she limped around to the path that would take her home, so she missed the expression on his face as he stood watching her pass. When she had disappeared he went slowly to the telephone.

Her knee had begun to ache, as it still did after a walk, and she was pleased to see the house, although the sky had clouded over and it looked raw and gaunt and secretive in its clearing. She built up the fire in the sitting room. The log basket was almost empty and she went out to where the wood was kept, split some logs with a hand axe, filled the basket, and carried it into the house. A sudden pain shot through her knee and left her gasping. She put the basket down and leaned against the wall, where Penny found her.

"It's your leg, isn't it?" she said anxiously. "You shouldn't be carrying weights like this." She picked up the basket. "I'll take it. I'm used to carrying. You ought to see the wood I carry at home."

They went into the sitting room and Penny built up the fire until it was burning brightly. "There," she said. "Now you sit down and rest your leg."

Rachel felt a flood of gratitude toward her. And she did not believe Penny had been mistaken in her story of the carriage incident. She had been too positive, repeated it too many times.

That evening, as she was preparing to take the girl home, the telephone rang. She felt as though a cold hand had closed over her heart. "I'll get it," she called. Her leg felt easier and as long as she did not put her weight on it, she could walk without pain. She went into Bill's room, closed the door, and lifted the receiver. This time she did not speak. There was a similar silence at the other end. But she was not as afraid as she had been on the previous occasions. Perhaps it had been her talk with Alec; perhaps he had done some good simply by listening. And then, abruptly, the silence was broken by a man's voice. It was muffled and had a metallic resonance. She had to strain to catch the words.

"You're losing your mind," the voice said. "You're becoming insane. There is only one way out. Do you want to go to an asylum? Do you want to spend the rest of your life among the mad?" The tones were hypnotic, insistent.

"No!" Rachel whispered. "No! No!"

She put the receiver down and thrust the telephone away. She put her hand across her mouth, pressing so tightly that she choked. She was shaking again, but this time with anger. How *dare* he! How dare *they!* No one, *no one* was going to invade her home like this. She began hobbling around the room, thinking furiously. She had to do something. She could not be passive; that wasn't in her nature. Fight back. That was the only way. But how? She didn't know *whom* to fight. Then she thought: California. If Bill was with Sally, that was the first thing she must know. Then other things would fall into place. So that's where she had to start. And Sophie could come with her.

She picked up the telephone again and called a travel agency in Chichester. They could get her on a British Airways flight leaving Heathrow at eleven o'clock in the morning in four days' time. But she wanted to go now, this minute. They were sorry, but the Christmas travel rush was already beginning.

"All right," she said, and gave the number of her credit card. "Book us."

She felt an immediate sense of relief at having done something positive. This time next week, she thought, I'll know. I'll find them. Wherever they are, I'll find them, and I'll know.

The four intervening days stretched ahead of her like an eternity. Could she hang on for four days and four nights? What about Sophie? Would she be in danger again? Would there be another attempt . . . ?

The idea came like an answer to a prayer: Penny could take Sophie. Rachel went to the bathroom where Penny was amusing the child with a floating plastic duck. When she mentioned her idea the round face cracked open with pleasure. "You mean take her home? Have her to myself? Why, I'd give anything . . ."

Penny lived on a smallholding with her mother and her brothers and sisters near the town of Addiscombe. From what she had said and from what Rachel had seen herself in her journeys back and forth each day, the Masons had come down in the world. When Penny's father was alive they had been able to make a living on their forty acres. They had kept a couple of cows, a couple of horses, raised hens, grown vegetables. But times had changed and now they struggled. The single-story house had been built by a developer in the fifties and was already beginning to fall to pieces.

Inside it was untidy and the furniture had been knocked about by children, and yet, unlike Mrs. Leech's cottage, there was a warmth, a welcome about the Mason place. Mrs. Mason was in her mid-forties and must once have been pretty. She was wearing a pair of skiing pants that had seen better days and a tight-fitting turtleneck sweater that emphasized her bust. She exuded a ripe sexuality. Her light-skinned features had a kind of serene comfortableness, and although she had several children of her own around she welcomed Sophie as though a new baby were the one thing she desired most of all.

"Ain't she lovely?" she said. "You come to stay with us, darling? You wait until my others see you. I won't get a look in." She picked Sophie out of the portable crib and swung the baby to her right hip with an easy, practiced motion. "There! What a big girl."

Rachel's excuse for the arrangement was that she was taking Sophie to America for Christmas and that she had to go to London before they left. Penny did not care what the reasons were. She followed Rachel into the house, her face shining with pleasure and anticipation.

They put Sophie down in a small, clean, warm room next to the kitchen. "Won't you have something?" Mrs. Mason said. "A drop of tea? Or there's some ginger wine."

"I'll make tea," Penny said urgently.

"All right, love," her mother said. "Make it good and strong."

She and Rachel chatted comfortably as though they had been friends for a long time. She gave a feeling of relaxation to the place and Rachel felt herself responding. Now she had met Mrs. Mason, her affair with Alec—if, indeed, the story was true—did not seem so squalid. His wife had been ill for years. It was not unnatural that he should turn to this warm, generous woman for comfort.

"I'm lucky to have Penny," she said.

"She loves being with you, Mrs. Chater. Sometimes I used to worry about her. She's a good girl but . . . you know . . . not too bright. Being with you has made all the difference to her. She really loves Sophie."

It was after seven when Rachel, regretfully, stood up. For a moment, looking down at Sophie lying peacefully in her little room, her left thumb in her mouth, she felt she could not bear to leave her. She caught her up and hugged her, then turned impulsively to Mrs. Mason to say she had changed her mind and would take the baby with her after all. But she tightened her mouth and handed Sophie to Penny.

"You—you'll look after her, won't you?" she said idiotically.

Mrs. Mason patted her arm. "We'll have a lovely time, dear," she said. "And it's better this way—you'll have lots to do before you go away and you'll get it all done quicker without having to worry about Sophie. You wait, the four days will pass in a flash."

Rachel smiled shakily, thanked her, and went out to her car.

17

She drove home slowly. She had purposely left all the lights on so she would not go back to a dark and gloomy house. It was lonely, but there was a compensating factor: she no longer felt quite so vulnerable. If anything happened to Sophie it would be far worse than anything that could happen to herself.

The telephone rang at nine o'clock. She walked deliberately into the study, picked it up, and then, without listening, set it back on its stand, breaking the connection. After a moment she took it off the hook and left it lying on the desk. Then she made sure the house was locked, went up to her bedroom, took two sleeping tablets, and passed out with her light still on.

She awoke slightly muzzy but with every muscle of her body relaxed and flaccid. She felt rested for the first time in weeks. The day stretched out before her. There were things she could be doing, but she had four days in which to do them.

She had a leisurely bath and went into the empty kitchen for a cup of coffee. Curiously, she found she was no longer frightened of the house. Even in broad daylight its dark corners had made her uneasy, but knowing that she would be escaping in a few days, she found herself looking around it almost with affection. She and Bill had been happy here. But now she had to anticipate confronting him in the company of his first wife, and if she did so, her own life with him, in this or any other house, would have ended. She felt tears rise as her mind's eye saw him suddenly, smiling down at her the way he had the day he had brought her home from the hospital. She remembered how eagerly she had limped up the steps toward the open door, where Nurse Griffin stood . . .

Nurse Griffin!

Her heart lurched as she remembered the woman's unsmiling eyes and tight mouth. She had never thought of Nurse Griffin! She had not bothered to hide her dislike of Rachel. She had shown no obvious affection for Sophie. She had left suddenly, in anger. Could *she* . . . ?

Quickly, Rachel reviewed what she knew of the nurse, and realized it was nothing more than that she had retired and lived in Chichester. She was a spinster in late middle-age. Strange things sometimes happened in the minds of such women. Mrs. Leech had talked about her resentment of Rachel's comfortable, protected life. Could Nurse Griffin, too, have resented it, and allowed her resentment to build up into such hatred that she would do anything to destroy the Chaters? If it *was* her, it would not alter the problem of Bill and Sally, but at least some of the happenings of the past weeks would be explained.

She went to the pile of telephone books on a shelf beside Bill's desk and pulled out the gray-green one labeled *Portsmouth and Isle of Wight,* which included Chichester. She ran her finger down the columns and there it was: Griffin, E.A., S.R.N., and a Chichester address.

It was a small bungalow on the far side of Chichester. The tiny garden was painfully neat and a few roses still struggled against the winter cold. Rachel rang the bell but did not hear any peal inside the house. She waited a few moments and pressed it again. No one answered.

A gravel path led around the house between the wintry rose beds, and she made her way to the back. Curtains were drawn on one of the windows and she thought she could see a chink of light between them. She went on past a small garden hut and a tiny vegetable patch where long-stemmed Brussels sprouts drooped in the cold.

She walked completely around the house and came back to the front door, where she stood uncertainly for a moment. She had steeled herself to come, had whipped up her courage on a froth of anger; and now there was no one to confront. Her anger was very near the surface and it burst out in a spurt as she thought of what Nurse Griffin might have been doing to her. Then, remembering the drawn curtains at one of the back windows, she banged with her hand on the glass panels of the door.

It could not have been quite closed, for it swung slowly open.

Dusk was already falling and the inside of the house was in semidarkness, except for a light at the end of the short passage. She wondered if the woman was there, ignoring her. Perhaps she had seen her from a window and decided not to answer the door, hoping Rachel would go away. Or was she ill? In bed?

Rachel looked about, but there seemed to be no one in the street, and the windows of the houses directly opposite were already curtained against the swiftly falling evening. She moved into the house.

"Nurse Griffin!" she called.

There was no answer.

Immediately to her right was the living room. She switched on the light. She was not an intruder, she told herself, she wanted everyone to know she was there. An anthracite fire burned against the far wall. The room, in shades of brown against dead white walls, with a dark, claret-colored carpet, was clinically tidy and impersonal. There was a lack of human warmth about it. The three matching pieces of furniture had wooden arms and looked uncomfortable. On a low table was a copy of the magazine *New Society*. The room told her nothing at all.

She went on down the passage. To the left was the kitchen, facing her a bathroom, and to the right of that a bedroom. She stopped in the doorway. It was the room she had seen from the outside. The curtains were drawn and the light by the bed was on. It seemed that Nurse Griffin had saved all her femininity and any frivolity that may have been in her character for this room.

Unlike the bare and impersonal living room, it was decorated in girlish pink and white; it was frilly and fluffy and seemed to bear no relationship to the grim, gray woman Rachel remembered.

On the satin counterpane was a toy giraffe, the kind that children unzip and stuff with their night clothes. From the ceiling hung a large mobile of Babar the Elephant. There was a chest of drawers and a wardrobe and a small, white-painted desk. It was the sort of room a child would have loved.

"Nurse Griffin!" Rachel said again, loudly, but the only answer was silence.

On top of the chest of drawers was a collection of small china animals that reminded her of the stage set for *The Glass Menagerie*.

Unlike the living room, the bedroom was not neat. A blouse was lying on the bed and a pair of houseshoes had been kicked off on the carpet. Against one wall was a pile of old magazines. She looked through the top copies. They were all called *Babycare*. On the desk lay a packet of cigarettes and a box of matches.

She had a sense of schizophrenia: if the Nurse Griffin she knew inhabited the living room, who lived in this pink and white nursery? Who lay in bed smoking and reading about babies and playing with little china animals?

She felt suddenly chilled. What else would this room tell her about Nurse Griffin? She opened the desk drawers but they contained only old bills and receipts, paper clips and rubber bands. The wardrobe, too, was just a wardrobe with dresses and skirts hanging in it. It was the chest of drawers that finally answered her questions.

The top drawers contained practical underwear, long warm nightgowns, thick stockings, and several starched white coats. She opened the bottom drawer and it was neatly filled with sweaters. She was about to close it when she saw underneath the sweaters a large cardboard box. She moved the clothes aside, pulled up a corner of the lid, and found herself looking at a pair of tiny white crocheted baby bootees.

Her hands were shaking as she pulled the box out onto the floor and opened it. It was filled with baby things: there were more booties, there were tiny, lacy nighties, there were little frocks with *broderie anglaise* on the front, there was a squashy teddy-bear. Her fingers darted in and out of the beautiful, laundered clothing.

And then they touched an envelope. She took it out and drew from it a series of old and yellowing newspaper cuttings. Her body went rigid as she read the headlines: BABY SNATCHED

IN PARKING LOT. And again: NO CLUE IN BABY SNATCH. POLICE CHIEF WARNS OF PSYCHOPATH. And again: SNATCHED BABY FOUND DEAD. And another: BABY-SNATCH MOTHER ATTEMPTS SUICIDE.

There were others, but as Rachel crouched to read them, she felt a draft on her legs, and turned. Nurse Griffin was standing behind her.

From Rachel's viewpoint, she looked huge. She was dressed for walking, in tweeds and heavy shoes, and carried a stick in her hand. Her short gray hair was shaped round her face like a Crusader's helm. They stared at each other for a second and then she took a step into the room.

"What are you doing here?" she said slowly.

Rachel rose to her feet, still clutching the newspaper clippings. She knew she had to get to the police. She was frightened, but she depended on her anger to keep her from falling apart. Remember what she did, she told herself.

"Well?"

She could not stop herself. "You tried to kill my baby!" she said.

"What?"

"Don't try to lie! You're insane! It says so here!" She shook the cuttings in Nurse Griffin's face and some of them fell to the floor. "You did it once before. You stole someone's baby. You killed it!"

For the first time the woman seemed to see the scattered baby clothes. She dropped her stick and knelt down. "How dare you!" she hissed. "How *dare* you touch those things!" She began to pick up the clothes and the cuttings, folding them as neatly as they had been before.

Unchecked, Rachel moved past her toward the door. But there was something in the way the older woman was behaving that made her hesitate. Nurse Griffin put the cuttings back in their envelope and tucked it under the baby clothes, closed the lid of the box, and replaced it where it had been. When she looked up Rachel could see that tears had squeezed under her thick pebble glasses and were running down her cheeks.

In a voice no louder than a whisper, she said, "It was *my* baby."

* * *

Rachel drove toward Addiscombe, sickened by the tragedy her suspicions of Nurse Griffin had uncovered. She had, stumblingly, tried to explain her actions, but the woman had simply stared at her, wet-faced, saying nothing, and after a few moments she had turned toward the door. As she went along the passage, Nurse Griffin had spoken, almost as though she were picking up an interrupted conversation. "I thought I was over it, you see, after all these years. But I wasn't. Your baby was the same age as *she* was when . . . So I left, because I couldn't bear it any longer." Then she had gone back into the nursery-bedroom, and closed the door behind her.

In Addiscombe Rachel stopped at the Masons. The entire family was in the sitting room. The television was on and they were loudly playing cards. In the center of the floor, chewing a cracker and unworried by the noise and the people, was Sophie.

For the next hour Rachel played with her daughter, drank tea, chatted, and felt normally cheerful for the first time in weeks. She was even able, for a time, to forget that she was no further ahead in her search for her persecutor.

18

Once again that night she unhooked the telephone and slept undisturbed. With neither Penny nor Sophie, the house the next day was huge and silent, but she kept herself occupied planning her travel wardrobe and the hours passed quickly as she sorted, washed, and ironed. It was not until early afternoon that she remembered she had forgotten to replace the telephone and felt a pang of apprehension as she realized that Mrs. Mason might have been trying to ring her about Sophie. But when she called all was well, and the rich Sussex accent was instantly comforting.

She was sitting at the kitchen table, sipping a cup of coffee, when the doorbell rang. She half expected to see Alec, but it was a delivery boy with an envelope in his hand. He gave it to her. "Chater?" he said. "Telegram. Tried to phone it, but there must be something wrong with your line. They couldn't get through."

"Oh . . . thank you."

She closed the door and turned the envelope in her hand. She had always hated telegrams. A telegram had brought her news of her father's death. Michael had sent telegrams more than once when he had been unable to leave his wife to meet her.

She walked slowly back to the table and tore it open. For a moment she could not believe her eyes and had to read it a second time: "Have been trying to ring you stop line constantly engaged stop am on my way home stop take care all love Bill."

Paralyzed by the flood of pure happiness that swept over her, it was minutes before she could think clearly and begin to work out what the telegram meant.

He was coming home. He had never meant to stay away. He had not met Sally in California. He probably did not even know she was there. As she had already suspected, the notes she had read were no more than that: notes for a novel. She, Rachel, had imagined the entire situation. Based on what? One casual remark by a woman who had known Sally—and, as she had said, not very well.

Alec had been right. Every single rational explanation he had produced for what had been happening must have been correct, including the suggestion that Penny's memory had been at fault. She had even suspected Celia! In her euphoria she could recognize the absurdity of that, for *no one* had been persecuting her. *Her* cat had been several cats. The phone calls were from some crank who had stumbled accidentally onto words to which she could relate.

"Am on my way home." When could she expect him? He had sent the telegram before leaving California but the time stamp was too blurred for her to make out. He could be back any time.

She ran upstairs, heedless of a warning pain in her knee, and began setting the bedroom to rights, dresses back in the wardrobe, underwear returned to drawers.

She found herself, for the first time in months, singing as she moved about the room, and by the time she had finished she had decided she must collect Sophie from the Masons. Bill would want to see her as soon as he arrived home.

Half an hour later she was sitting with Mrs. Mason in the cheerful, crowded cottage, while Penny, somewhat downcast at the unexpected ending of her idyll, gathered the baby's things together.

"I never saw such a difference in anyone, dear!" Mrs. Mason said. "I was quite worried about you last night, you were so pale and worried. Now look at you. There's nothing like a man, is there?"

Rachel laughed. "I never realized how much I'd miss my husband."

"It's a lonely house, that one of yours. Penny's told me about it. She says you haven't even got any near neighbors."

"Alec Webb is the nearest . . ." Rachel stopped, remembering that Mrs. Mason would know all too well where he lived. But Penny's mother looked only mildly interested.

"That's the vet, isn't it?" she said. "We called him in a few times when he lived here. Seemed a nice man. Pity about his eyes. Someone told me he was going blind. Has it happened yet?"

Rachel stared at her. "Not quite, he can still see a little. I thought you knew him."

"Not really. Only through the animals, like. He'd known my husband's family for years, though. I knew his wife better. She used to come to our Women's Institute meetings regular."

"You knew her better than you knew him?"

"Much better. I don't suppose I met him more than three times."

Rachel hesitated. "Was this before or after your husband died?"

"He came a couple of times when I was by myself. Then I had to get rid of the animals. They were a bit much for me without George."

Could she be lying? Her blue eyes were without guile, her manner so natural that it could not be feigned. Rachel was conscious, not for the first time, of the viciousness of village gossip: a vet calls twice on an attractive widow to minister to her ailing animals and instantly the rumor of an affair between them is born . . . and survives even years later. Celia had been vague about where she had heard it, but even she, by passing it on to Rachel, was helping to keep it alive.

"He was very good to our Penny, though," Mrs. Mason was saying. "Recommending her for the job with you, and all. Will you still be wanting her when your husband's home, Mrs. Chater?"

"I couldn't do without her—and neither could Sophie."

This did a little to comfort Penny, but there were still tears in her eyes as she saw them off a few minutes later.

Rachel had not been back in the house more than half an hour when, once again, the doorbell rang.

Still expecting Alec, she rehearsed her news on the way downstairs. She flung open the door. "Alec! Bill's . . ." She stopped.

Celia was standing there, tall and elegant in a green suede coat with a mink scarf tucked in the neck.

"Oh, I'm sorry! I was half expecting Alec." She felt a sudden constraint, but Celia was smiling.

There was little warmth in Rachel's polite nod. She was remembering the gossip about Alec—which, she recalled guiltily, she had been all too willing to believe.

"You were upset about the ring," she said. "It was all a mistake."

"A stupid one, and my fault entirely. I'd like to apologize to Penny, too. Is she here?"

"No. I've just been to her place to fetch Sophie. She and Mrs. Mason have been looking after her. Penny will be here tomorrow."

"Then I'll come again."

Looking suddenly forlorn, she turned to leave, and Rachel realized that she would be returning to an empty cottage. "Come in," she said impulsively. "It isn't too early for a drink, is it?"

"I'd love to," Celia said promptly. "But it's not much after five. How about tea?"

As she was taking her coat off, Rachel could not contain herself: "Celia, Bill's on his way home!"

Celia was unwinding her scarf and it was a second before she replied. "How lovely for you. But I thought he wasn't due for some time."

"So did I, but I had a telegram a couple of hours ago. He'd been trying to ring me but I'd taken the telephone off the hook because of some damn anonymous caller and he couldn't get through."

"When do you expect him?"

"Tomorrow at the latest, I hope."

"Then I mustn't stay too long. You'll be wanting to get things ready for him. How about your other problems—the cat? And those calls?"

She shrugged. "The calls were from some nut. The cat? Pure imagination on my part. I guess it was a sort of delayed shock after the car accident. As soon as I knew Bill was coming home, everything fell into perspective. Anyway, enough of that. Have you seen anything of Alec lately?"

"Why do you ask?"

"Because I've just heard something about Alec that you should know. Celia, you remember that gossip about him and Penny's mother?"

"What gossip?"

"You must remember! You told me you'd heard that she had been his mistress."

"Did I? Oh, yes, of course. Most people seem to know about it."

"It isn't true."

"What do you mean?"

"Mrs. Mason barely knows Alec. He knew her husband's family, but she only saw him a few times when he came to her farm as a vet."

"How did you find this out? Surely you didn't tell her what I said?"

"Of course I didn't. His name came up in conversation and she said she'd known his wife far better than she had known him."

"I suppose she would say that, wouldn't she?"

"No, she wouldn't! I absolutely believed her. She isn't the kind of woman to lie."

Celia's face softened suddenly and she held out her hand in an appealing gesture. "Oh lord, Rachel! And I passed on that silly story I'd heard. What must you think of me? I don't often gossip —I think perhaps I was feeling just a little upset about Alec. You know, finding out that he was an ordinary man after all. I'd admired him so much."

"Well, now you can forget it. Aren't you pleased?"

"Delighted!" Her face lit up as she smiled and Rachel felt the force of her charm. Uncomfortably, she remembered what she had said to Alec. Fortunately he had not appeared to take her suspicions seriously. Looking at Celia's calm, beautiful features, she realized anew how grotesque her fantasies had been.

"I haven't seen him for a while," Celia said sadly. "He seems to have been avoiding me, for some reason."

"Now that's *your* imagination!" Rachel said.

Celia smiled, but she changed the subject and they chatted comfortably over their tea until she stood up to leave. It was just after six. As she reached the front door she said, casually, "So you've lost your fear of the cat, have you?"

"More or less. I just hope the wretched thing is dead. Alec says it was my feelings of guilt about Charlie, and having injured it, that made me imagine it was deliberately terrorizing me."

"Oh, it isn't dead," Celia said. "I saw it on the snow near those rhododendrons of yours as I drove in. It's a huge creature."

A cold finger, a residue of fear, seemed to touch Rachel's heart.

"Where did it go?"

"Under the bushes. It's clearly crippled. Funny thing, it actually seemed to be watching the house. Still, you can always get Bill to shoot it for you, can't you? See you soon. 'Bye."

The cat had passed into a state where even its highly developed brain had difficulty functioning in any active way, though the flame of instinct still flickered in its conscious mind. Its body, too, was only half alive. Its back legs were almost paralyzed and when it moved it had to pull itself on its front paws.

It had been lying near the rhododendron bush for two days without food.

It was a bitterly cold evening. Powder snow had fallen and a northeasterly gale was blowing, bringing in icy air from Russia. The wind had blown snow under the bush and was piling it against the cat's body.

The house represented something in its brain. It could not know that it was a pattern from the past, for it could not have analyzed the stimuli. But the stimuli were there nevertheless: warmth, safety. They triggered off a response in its brain and it began to drag itself over the thin coating of snow toward the house. It sought entry by the front, but there was none. It turned the corner and slowly moved along the side of the house. A scent of food, coming through the cellar window, was reaching it.

Then the headlights of Celia's car swept around the drive, and fear, even stronger than hunger, sent it back to its shelter.

Much later, when the snow turned to rain, it emerged again.

19

Rachel wished Celia had not mentioned the cat. Its behavior was the one thing about which Alec's rational explanations were still not entirely convincing. If Celia was right and it had been the same cat she had injured, the theory that she had seen several different creatures did not stand up. And it would be difficult to mistake *the* cat because of its unnatural size.

She remembered, and it gave her comfort, that the shotgun in the cellar was still set ready to fire. She had told Alec to leave it, as nobody went near the area outside the mesh window. When Bill came home he could dismantle it and find some other way to get rid of the cat.

She shook off her misgivings and decided to pour herself a drink. As she crossed the sitting room with her glass she caught sight of herself in the mirror above the fireplace and thought, with surprise, You're a different person! The shadow behind her eyes had gone, her face was flushed and animated, her mouth curved up in a smile. She raised her glass to the reflection and said aloud, "And this is the last time you and I will be drinking alone. Thank God!"

She sat in front of the fire, sipping her drink and planning. Bill would telephone from the airport. He would probably take the train to Chichester and she could pick him up there.

There was a tapping on the window. She sat as though turned to stone. Silence collected in the room. Had it been her imagination? It came again. Tap . . . tap . . . tap . . . the way it always started in the dream. She found herself locked into a state of shock, listening not only with her ears, but with every part of her body. Tap . . . tap . . . tap. It was insistent, like the ringing of the telephone, demanding to be answered, demanding to be investigated.

Almost in a trance, she found herself moving toward the closed curtains as though drawn on a length of string. Her hands went up and she jerked them aside. She had known all along what she would see. There was Charlie's face, hair plastered down by the rain, the blood trickling from the forehead. The eyes . . . the eyes . . . the scream burst from her throat and shattered the silence, and came again and again as she stood with her hands to her cheeks, staring at this monstrous thing in the night.

Then, as the first shock wore off, she saw there was something wrong with the face. The eyes were wrong—nor was it the cat's face she had seen before. She leaned forward, stared through the rain-driven glass, and found herself looking at a tailor's dummy on which a face had been crudely drawn under a dark wig. It was a trick. A game. She whirled around, but there was no one in the room behind her.

Tap . . . tap . . . tap.

It couldn't be. How could a dummy . . . ? She turned again and this time there were two faces at the window, the second a frightening, patchwork thing, distorted even more by the rain on the windows. It was Alec.

"Oh God," she whispered. She pulled the curtains closed with a snap. Hysteria and panic had her by the throat. She backed away from the windows toward the study, toward the telephone from which she could call the police.

Alec! The name repeated itself over and over. It had been Alec all the time!

She was half way across the floor when she heard a man's voice. It spoke slowly and clearly: "First the tapping. It came above the rain and the wind. Just a tapping. At the window."

She screamed again, for the voice was as familiar to her as her own. It was Bill's voice. She ran toward the hall and at that moment all the lights in the house went off. She fled blindly from the sitting room, panic pumping the adrenalin into her muscles. She found herself in the hall. The front door was locked—but the key had gone. She ran to the kitchen and the back passage where Franco had had his basket. That door, too, was locked and the key was gone. She stood in the passage, her heart hammering in her ears, casting about her like a fox brought to bay. All the windows on the ground floor had burglarproof locks. She needed a key to open them. She could not think where it was.

But first she had to get Sophie, who was sleeping in her room upstairs. She had to take Sophie away from this house.

She stood in the darkness trying to clear her mind, trying to formulate some sort of plan. It was her house. She knew it well. That was all she had in her favor. The telephone. She dared not go back to the one downstairs. But there was an extension in her bedroom. Sophie. Then the telephone. She listened, but the house was silent.

She went to the back staircase, stopped, listened again, then slowly began to go up. Suddenly there was a tremendous crash of glass from somewhere near the kitchen. A scream rose into her throat again but she managed to choke it down. Ignoring the sudden pain in her knee, she ran up to Sophie's room and reached into the crib. It was empty. And then an animal cry escaped her lips. Desperately, she ran her hands over the rumpled sheets in case the baby was curled up in a corner, but as she did so she knew it was no use. Sophie was gone. Hang on, she told herself. You can't give way now. Think! As silently as she could, she left the room, ran to her own bedroom and picked up the telephone. It came away in her hand. The wire had been cut.

One word kept hammering in her mind: help! You must have help. Whatever is happening, you can't cope with it alone. She heard again Mrs. Mason's words: "It's a lonely house . . . you haven't even got any near neighbors . . ." And she had said, "Alec Webb is the nearest . . ." But Alec was part of this. It must have been Alec who had taken Sophie . . .

None of the upstairs windows were burglarproofed and the one in the spare room opened onto the roof of the front porch. She might be able to clamber onto it and climb down to the ground. Because the first essential was to get out; to find help somewhere. She crossed the hall, let herself into the spare room, and closed the door. She tried to lock it but this key, too, had been removed.

The window opened easily. The porch roof seemed ominously

far below. If she could get her body over the sill and hang by her hands she might just be able to reach it with her toes and once there—

It was no more than a whisper, but she heard it clearly. Bill said, "Jump! Why don't you jump?" His voice was warm and friendly and had an almost hypnotic quality. The shock caused her to teeter on the windowsill. She drew back and swung around. A figure was standing in the doorway. "Do you want to spend your life with mad people?" Bill said. "This is your chance. Take it now. Jump."

A flashlight beam flickered over the walls of the landing and picked out the figure in the doorway. For a second it was brightly lit, and Rachel saw that it was Celia. She was dressed in jeans and a parka. In her left hand she held Bill's dictating machine and in the other a meat knife, one of Rachel's own Sabatiers from the kitchen, with a blade six inches long. Tucked under her left arm, hugged to her ribs, head lolling, was Sophie's small, limp body.

For a second, Rachel was rigid, then her legs began to shake and she could only hold out her arms and whisper, "Don't . . ."

At that moment another voice said, "You bloody bitch!" It was Alec and he, too, was coming up the stairs toward her, holding a flashlight.

Before she could move, he tripped. She heard him stumble and the flashlight gyrated wildly for a moment before it went out. She heard it roll down the stairs. Her strength returned with a rush and in that second, when Celia's attention was diverted, she grabbed up a pillow from the bed, flung it at Celia's head, and launched herself forward. In the darkness she collided with the other woman and snatched her baby. She raced from the room. At the top of the stairs she ran into another body. It was Alec, getting to his feet. She was vaguely conscious that he reached for her, but she swerved and went down the stairs, hearing above her the sound of shouting and violent movement. Her foot touched something. It was the flashlight and she scooped it up.

She had no idea what was happening, only that she must find safety for Sophie and herself. The child's body was soft and relaxed and she heard herself whispering over and over again,

"Oh God, let her be all right!" She reached the ground floor and heard them on the stairs behind her.

She had to get out, but how? They had locked the doors. Then she remembered the cellar. It was the one door in the house that had no lock. It had a bolt on the house side, but also a bolt on the cellar side, from the days before the back section of the house had been added, when the door had opened into the garden. She ran through the passages, reached the door, and flung it open. She felt for the steep, plunging steps, then closed the door behind her, throwing the rusty bolt into its socket. She slithered down into the cellar, now bathed in silvery moonlight. She heard the handle of the door turn. Then a body banged into it. But the bolt had held for thirty years and held now. She heard the bolt on the other side being slid into its socket. While there was no way into the cellar, there was also no way out. A heavy black cloud crossed the moon and the room was plunged into darkness so thick that she could see nothing. She was about to switch on the flashlight, but stopped herself. They might see the beam through a crack in the door and they did not know she had the flashlight; it could give her an advantage. The freezer was over to her right, the boiler to her left. Ahead she could make out the overgrown screen and the bars at the window as a lighter shade of dark. She knew that underneath the window was the coal chute and she knew the cat food was still there, for while she could not see it, she could smell it.

She began to feel her way across the cellar toward the freezer. After what seemed like minutes, but could only have been seconds, she touched it. She crouched in the angle between the freezer and the wall, where the cat had hidden the night she had surprised it.

Gently, she laid Sophie on the floor and ran her hands over the tiny body. It was cold under the flannelette nightgown, but the heart was beating and, in the silence, she could hear short, sobbing breaths.

The cloud passed the moon and the components of the cellar became visible, though not as clearly as before. She looked at the window. A figure was bending down toward it, cutting the moonlight.

"Now where will you run?" Celia said.

She kept quite still, knowing that in her hiding place she could not be seen.

"Come out, come out, wherever you are," Celia said, imitating a child's voice. And then she laughed. "Poor Rachel! Did you like my game of hide-and-seek? I haven't played it since I was a child. I hope Sophie enjoyed it, too. I had to give her something to make her sleep, so perhaps she didn't, after all. But we'll play other games—I have such plans for her. Talking of plans, don't you think the recorder was a stroke of genius? I could use Bill's voice whenever I liked. All those telephone calls. They were fun, too. I wanted you to get just a hint that the voice was Bill's. The merest feeling. I didn't want to spoil the grand finale. I've planned it for so long."

So *she* had taken the tapes, Rachel thought.

As if reading her mind, Celia said, "I found the tapes weeks ago. I've been all over your house. You heard me the first time, remember? I could tell how frightened you were. I watched you closing the larder window. Silly Rachel. Then I used to come in during those walks you took, when Penny was playing with the child. She didn't have a clue. I've watched you almost every day, and you never knew. I even saw you looking for the tapes in Bill's room. But I had them by then. I'd edited them by then. Just the bits I wanted. It's fascinating, you know . . ." The words trailed off.

Why? Rachel said to herself. Why?

The voice started again. "I used to play games with my mother. Hide-and-seek, in a house much bigger than this. I would hide and she would seek. And once *she* hid." The voice was dreamy, with a far-off quality, as though Celia were talking to herself, reminding herself of the past. "I was frightened of that house. Frightened of her. Just as you are frightened of me. Once I hid in a cupboard and she locked the door and pretended to go away. I could hear her starting the car outside. But it was only a tease, you see, because I had been untidy. Now *you* are the one who is hiding, and I am seeking—and finding."

Rachel was stung into speech. "*What do you want?*"

"Ah, so you *were* there. I thought you must be. The young Mrs. Chater. Wife of the well-known novelist. Such a handsome couple. With such a lovely daughter. *Now* look at you!" She laughed.

"*What do you want?*"

"You," Celia said.

"Me? But why me? What have I ever done to you?"

"Don't you remember your Bible? 'Eye for eye, tooth for tooth, hand for hand, foot for foot, burning for burning, wound for wound, stripe for stripe . . .' You see, I know it all."

Celia rattled the window bars as though trying to break them. "You had your chance upstairs," she said. "Why didn't you take it?" She beat at the bars with a dead branch but made no impression. Frustrated, her voice was harsh when she spoke again. "You thought you had it all, didn't you? You stupid American bitch. The whole bloody lot. My husband . . . my baby . . . the lot!"

Rachel was confused. "What husband? What baby? You're mad!"

"That's what they tried to say, but it isn't true. They killed *my* baby! Eye for eye . . . don't you see?"

"It was *you!* You tried to kill Sophie!"

There was a pause. "That went wrong, didn't it?" Celia said in a softer voice. "You came down too soon. And I even thought of the scratches on the carriage. Clever Celia. My mother always knew I was clever. She never said so, but she knew."

"You're insane!" She had said the same thing to Nurse Griffin. This time she knew she was right.

Celia laughed. "We'll see. We'll see. Now don't go away, will you?"

Rachel heard her footsteps fade away; but then they seemed to merge with another sound.

Tap . . . tap . . . tap.

She pressed back against the wall, trying to make herself as small as possible.

Tap . . . tap . . .

She covered her ears with her hands, but it was no use. Although the tapping was faint, it penetrated her hearing.

"Rachel!" The voice was hollow, as though coming from the bottom of a well; little more than a whisper, filled with a strange, ghostly resonance. There was something desperate and despairing about it. "For God's sake, help me!" It was coming from the cellar door. She looked up at the window, but Celia had not returned. Softly she crossed the cellar and climbed the stairs. As she reached the top the voice said again, "Rachel!"

It was Alec. She knelt on the steps and placed her ear against the door panels. She could hear him breathing, a ragged, stertorous sound.

"Alec?" she whispered.

He groaned. Then her hand touched something sticky. She jerked away and switched on the flashlight. A dark pool of blood had formed on the top step and was dripping onto the next. It was seeping under the cellar door.

"Help me!" Alec said.

For a few moments she did not move. What if Celia was out there? She thought, What if the blood was not blood, but was part of the game, too? Then she remembered the knife in Celia's hand and Alec's voice shouting, "You bloody bitch!" She had assumed he was shouting at her, but it must have been at Celia. And then . . . what? Had Celia used the knife on Alec? If so, then Alec was on *her* side. She slipped the bolt and heard the one on the other side click back. She switched on the flashlight and opened the door.

Alec was on his knees, facing her, his hands clutching the right side of his neck. Blood was spilling over in a rivulet, running down his arms and chest and forming a pool on the floor.

"Oh Jesus!" Rachel whispered.

As she helped him to his feet she realized he was pressing on the edges of the wound to close it. He swayed as, slowly, she brought him down the steps and closed the door behind him, making sure the bolt went home. He sank onto the cellar floor.

Panting with the effort, she ripped a seam of her light woolen skirt and wound a strip of it around his neck like a scarf, trying to keep the lips of the wound closed.

"Sophie?" he whispered.

"She's here."

"Thank God! Can we—get out? Where's Celia?"

"I don't know. She was at the window, then she went away."

"Are you—ready?" His voice was soft and hoarse, as though the wound had damaged his vocal cords.

She picked up the baby, who whimpered in her drugged sleep.

"It's all right, darling," Rachel whispered. *"You're* all right. We're getting out."

When she reached Alec again, he was on his hands and knees.

"Hurry," he whispered. "She'll be back."

"How can you be sure?"

"Because I know her now. We've got to get away!"

"Can you walk?"

"Help me up."

She slipped her free arm under his so she could heave him to his feet. He draped an arm around her shoulders and she could hear his breathing, like strangled sobs, in her ear. He was not a tall man, but he was thickset and heavy and she seemed to be bearing his full weight.

Clutching Sophie, she put her foot on the first step, terrified she might hear Celia at the door. Alec, supporting himself on one side against the wall, moved with her. They had reached the third step when the uneven distribution of weight on her injured leg caused her knee to twist as she tried to keep her balance. Pain shot through her body, and it was as though the leg became jelly. It buckled under her and she felt herself falling. She let Alec go and twisted her body to protect the baby as she landed on the floor. When she regained her breath the pain in her leg was like fire but, as far as she could tell, she was otherwise unhurt.

"Where are you?" she whispered desperately.

She felt Alec move, heard him whisper, "Here." She tried to stand but, again, the leg would not support her. There was no question of her mounting the stairs, with or without Alec.

She was shivering. "Alec, what's going to happen to us?"

He did not reply and for a moment she thought he had lapsed into unconsciousness. She flicked the flashlight on and off. His eyes were open and he was staring past her at nothing. Sophie was whimpering more loudly now and Rachel could only welcome the sounds as proof that she was gaining strength. She put her on the floor again.

"Alec . . ."

"I told myself it was your imagination," he said. "I told myself that it was a reaction to your accident. I told myself all sorts of things . . ."

"It was Celia? All the time?"

His head was against her arm and she felt him nod. The strange, whispering voice went on: ". . . by yourself. Knew you were by yourself so I . . . so I came down and then . . . then I saw the thing at the window . . ."

"The dummy?"

"It was hers. I knew, you see . . . in her bedroom . . . for dressmaking."

Rachel had a vision of Alec and Celia in bed, the dummy standing in a corner of the room, watching them.

He said, so softly she could hardly hear, "My fault . . . I wouldn't believe it . . . could have stopped . . ."

"Alec, when did you know?"

"The dead cat."

"In the road? What . . . ?"

"Whatever you said, I *knew* it hadn't been there before. Only Celia . . . I took the body home . . . not run over . . . strangled. It had been dead for days . . . recognized it then. It was one of hers."

"Hers? I didn't know she had a cat."

"She had two . . . then only one. Said the other had . . . run away. But I wouldn't believe . . ." His voice faded away.

"Alec? Alec?"

"Came . . . to see you . . . locked. Saw her . . . inside. Had to break a window . . . too late to stop her taking Sophie . . . heard Bill's voice . . . followed her . . . knife . . ."

"Alec!"

But he did not answer.

The cat had pulled itself along the side of the house toward the window that represented safety and food, the only two instincts remaining in its flickering brain. The hole in the mesh was more than a foot off the ground and it could not pull itself up. It tried twice and then its strength gave out and it lay in the darkness at the base of the window. There were footsteps on the gravel. Tiny electrical impulses in what was left of its brain warned it to get away and it began to gather itself for the effort.

"Are you still there, Rachel?" The voice was mocking now.

The moon had come up from behind the clouds and Rachel could see Celia's figure outlined at the window. Then she smelled a well-known smell and realized what was happening: Celia was pouring kerosene through the window and down the coal chute. It ran onto the floor and began to form a small pool.

"Celia! For God's sake . . . !"

"For whose sake? Never heard of him. For Bill's sake. For Charlie's sake. Yes, that's more like it."

"Charlie!"

"You weren't content with Bill. You had to have Charlie too."

"That's a lie!"

"Do you think I believe that? You wanted him. You led him on. Do you think I believed all that rubbish about how he tried to rape you?"

"It was *you!*" Rachel said. "You were the one he was having an affair with. Mrs. Leech knew there was someone. She thought it was me. But it was you. When he was supposed to be working for you."

"Clever Rachel. Clever, clever Rachel! My God, it took you long enough. Yes, me. We only had ten days. Then you killed him."

"I didn't . . ."

"I don't care how. You killed him. Eye for eye, Rachel . . ."

"It was an accident!"

Celia ignored her. "People think you can simply strike a match and light kerosene," she said, conversationally.

Suddenly, Rachel felt Alec's hand on her arm. "The gun!" he whispered.

She had completely forgotten the shotgun clamped to the beam, but as soon as she tried to rise to her feet, she knew her leg would never stand it. "My knee! I can't," she whispered back.

"They're always doing it in the movies," Celia went on. Rachel strained her eyes, but could not make out what she was doing. "A tin of the stuff, a match and, whoosh, a whole building gone."

"Keep her talking," Alec said. "I'll try . . ."

". . . nonsense," Celia said. "It won't light. You must have kindling. I found this out years ago, all by myself."

Alec began to pull himself along the floor, dragging his body through the pool of kerosene.

"Celia, please listen!" Rachel wasn't sure what she was going to say, only that she had to go on talking.

But Celia was lost in her own thoughts. "Wood shavings make good kindling. I found some in the shed. Hope you don't mind."

The kerosene had reached Rachel and was soaking into her clothing. Again she tried to stand, but could not.

Her eyes had become accustomed to the darkness and she could see that Alec was now just below the gun. Instead of pulling himself upright against the freezer, he crawled on, and she realized he was making for the chute and the string, which, if he could grasp it, would set off the charge.

"This isn't the way I planned it," Celia went on. "But it'll do. Charred bodies of young mother and child found in burnt house. What *could* have happened?"

"Do you think the police are fools?" Rachel said.

Alec had managed to reach the chute.

"The police? Why should they investigate?" Celia said. "These old houses. Something must have gone wrong with the wiring. What about suicide? Balance of the mind disturbed. She had been acting strangely lately. Thought a cat was haunting her. A cat? Yes, a cat. Such a shame. And so young. There. That's just about right."

Below Celia's line of vision Alec was pulling himself upright against the chute, reaching his hand toward the string. And then Rachel saw something was wrong. In his semiblindness, in the dark of the cellar, he was reaching to the wrong side of the window, his hand a foot away from the line of the string.

"Alec!" she hissed.

Startled, he jerked backwards, did not have the strength to recover, and fell.

"Alec! Are you all right?" She heard him struggling to his feet, and she remembered the flashlight. His voice echoed in her mind from the hours they had spent in the cellar, waiting for the cat:

". . . aim it at the tear in the mesh. Only way I can see with this bloody eye." If she could illuminate the string for him now . . .

She switched on the flashlight. Celia was leaning forward, her face witchlike, about to strike a match and light the wood shavings. Below her, on the floor, lay Alec. The light no longer mattered to him. And then she saw the eyes, cat's eyes, flaring in the light of the flashlight.

Invisible as it crouched below the window, the cat had stayed where it was even when the woman had piled her shavings beside its body.

But the flashlight provided the shock that finally roused it into one last effort at self-preservation. Hissing, it launched itself upwards, claws extended, straight into Celia's face. She screamed and beat at the bundle of black fur. As she struggled, she fell forward; her elbow went through the hole in the mesh and pushed against the string.

There was a roar as the shotgun went off and the cat and the woman flew backwards.

In the cellar, Rachel was deafened by the noise and her nose was filled with cordite fumes.

As the echoes of the blast died down she heard a voice shouting, "Rachel! Rachel!" It was coming from outside. She heard feet running on gravel.

"Rachel! Where the hell are you? Are you all right?"

Bill had come home.

20

"That's what I can't seem to take in," she said. "That Celia was *Sally*."

She was sitting with Bill in front of the fire. Their arms were intertwined, their fingers laced, as though subconsciously they were locking onto each other like vines. It was dawn, but neither of them felt like sleep. Instead, they had made a huge pot of coffee and laced it with brandy. The police and ambulances had gone. Celia's body had been removed for an autopsy and Alec had been rushed to an intensive-care unit in Chichester. Sophie, after a medical examination, was upstairs, sleeping off the effects of antihistamine tablets.

Bill and Rachel had made separate statements to the police. Now, to each other, they went over them again and again, trying to make sense of the situation. They had finished the first pot of coffee and made another. They smoked too many cigarettes. They talked and talked, but through it all, Rachel was conscious that there were gaps. She noticed that Bill avoided mentioning Celia and she wondered, painfully, whether it was because he had been so much in love with her that he could not bear even to discuss her.

There was a silence then, suddenly, he said, "I've never talked about Sally to anyone before."

"You don't have to . . ."

"I should have told you when we first met, then all this might have been avoided. It was my fault. I *knew* her, but I kept trying to convince myself that it was all over. I should have guessed it wasn't, not for her, anyway."

Rachel tightened her hand on his. He was staring into the fire and turned to smile at her briefly.

"It started when I was twenty-one and she was twenty," he said. "We met at a party in London. She was extraordinarily pretty and charming. She was an actress—not a very successful one, but I saw her in rep several times and she wasn't bad. The main thing was, she had a genuine ability to take on different personalities according to the parts she played."

Bill Chater, the young writer who had just finished his first book, fell in love with the girl who had been introduced to him as Sally James, and they were married a few weeks later.

He said bitterly, "A month after we were married I discovered she was a pathological liar. She made up stories for the fun of it and lived a kind of fantasy life, moving in and out of different characters as she felt inclined. At first I forgave her everything, because she was an actress. I was pretty naive: I thought all actresses behaved like that. She even took different names according to the personality she had assumed. The first thing that made me suspicious of her was when we were in York—she was doing a play there and I was happy, at that stage, to be playing the devoted husband who trailed after her. We ran into a chap in the street who greeted her as 'Celia,' when I had always known her as Sally. She passed that off by saying that Sally was a family nickname which she preferred. Then other things began to impinge. She was a great partygoer and hated staying at home in the evening. Inevitably, I met more and more of her acquaintances and sometimes when I talked to them they mentioned facts about her background which simply didn't jell with what she had told me. For instance, she had said her mother and father had left England when she was eighteen to live in the States, where her father was a film producer. She even said she had sent him a copy of my book, with a recommendation that it would make a great screenplay, and claimed to have had a letter back from him saying he liked the idea, suggesting that we should join him in Hollywood and that she would be perfect for the lead."

Rachel looked at him in disbelief. "You believed that?"

"I was twenty-one. I didn't know anything about movies. I thought myself that the book would translate well into a screenplay—and she was so bloody convincing. We waited and waited to hear from America again, and then I learned from one of her friends that the parents as she had described them simply didn't exist. He told me that as far as he knew her father was a professor of geology at Edinburgh University."

"Didn't you ask her about all this?"

"Of course I did. She laughed and said she enjoyed claiming distinguished parents and that in fact hers were rather dull Londoners who lived in Streatham. Her father worked for the local council."

"Was that true?"

"No. Anyway, until about six months after the wedding I still thought the lies were harmless enough, mainly because she admitted them when I asked her about them. I was even amused by all the different Christian names she had adopted. As far as I was concerned, she remained Sally."

"What was her real name?"

"The one you knew: Celia James."

"Did she revert to her maiden name after your divorce?"

"Yes, on the whole, though she used Chater when it suited her. As time went on, other things began to happen and they were more serious than making up names or parents. She'd steal; take money out of my pockets and then deny it. She sold my silver cigarette case, but blamed our cleaning woman for having stolen it."

"She tried something like that with Penny."

"I began to watch her more carefully and after a while I realized something: I'd been doing research on psychopaths for a novel and, Christ, here was one in my own house! She was a classic case. No remorse, no conscience, erratic behavior, amoral attitudes. It was all there. And yet, even after I knew it, there were times when her charm was irresistible."

"She said she'd had a baby. Was that a lie?"

"No, it was real enough," he said bleakly. "It was a mistake, of course. By the time I knew what she was, the last thing I wanted her to be was the mother of my child. But once she was pregnant, there was nothing I could do about it. She refused to have an abortion. In fact, she became obsessed by her unborn child.

Her whole life centered around it. She related everything to it: the food she ate, drinking, smoking, walking, everything . . ." His voice trailed off.

"Did she ever go to a psychiatrist?"

"God, no! I suggested that after one of the stealing episodes and she was so mad she attacked me with a meat skewer."

"What happened after the baby was born?"

"It was three weeks premature, a girl. They put her in an oxygen tent because, like a lot of premature babies, she had a respiratory problem. But apparently there's also a problem with an oxygen tent. If you keep a baby in too long it can go blind, if you take it out too soon it can have breathing difficulties. In this case, the doctors made the wrong decision. They took her out of the tent and she died twenty-four hours later. Sally went off her head. She accused the hospital of murder and then attacked one of the nurses with a pair of scissors. Bloody nearly killed the woman. So they put her away in a psychiatric ward until she had got over it.

"When she came home, things went from bad to worse. She'd already started to sleep around. Now she didn't even try to cover up. She went after any man in sight. Once I found her in bed with the chap who had come to fix the dishwasher." He reached for the pot and poured himself another cup of coffee. "I'd had enough by then and at that time she seemed to want a separation, so I left her and, finally, divorced her."

"Did you ever see her again?"

"All too often. Soon after the divorce she began to haunt me, out of pure malice. I suspect one of her love affairs had gone wrong and that turned her spite back on me. She would wait for me outside my flat. She even used to go to my publishers and tell them the most appalling lies about me."

"Why didn't you have her put away?"

"Oh, hell, I couldn't! She'd been my wife . . . I was desperately sorry for her. I ran away instead. Took off for the States. I'd only been there a couple of months when I heard she'd been picked up for shoplifting in Harrod's and had thrown acid at the store detective. So they put her away again for observation and then they sent her to Rapley."

"Rapley?"

"It's a psychiatric unit in Yorkshire. I came back to England soon after that and one day I got a call from the superintendent of the unit saying she had been asking to see me. He said it might do her some good if I went. But when I got there, she wouldn't speak to me. They put the two of us in a private room and she just sat there, looking out of the window. I remember it was winter and snow on the ground. Very bleak. I tried and tried to get through to her but she only stared out at the snow. Then when I was leaving she smiled at me in that way she had, sort of—"

"Mocking."

"Yes. And she said, 'The baby wasn't yours, of course.' That was all. I left."

"Oh, darling . . ."

"I found out something else while I was there. She had told me once that she had been born in York. It was just after my second book had come out and the publishers were sending me cuttings of reviews. One had come in from the Yorkshire *Echo*. It was bloody good and I couldn't resist showing it to her. That was a mistake. She was jealous of any publicity I received. She read it and tossed it back to me and said something like, 'You think that miserable little paragraph's something—you should have seen the amount of space that paper gave *us!*' I asked what she meant, but she wouldn't explain. I thought it was another of her fantasies but after I'd been to see her I remembered it. I had a few hours to kill in York before catching the train back to London so I went to the local newspaper morgue. The old librarian remembered the case well and found the files. It was all there. She and her mother—the father was dead—had lived alone in a house outside the city. One day a fire broke out. By the time firemen arrived it was damaged beyond repair. Sally was found crouching under a bush outside and was taken away by a local social worker. Incidentally, she did the rest of her growing up in a variety of foster homes. When the firemen could get into the house, they came across a locked cupboard under the stairs. They opened it and found the body of Sally's mother. Sally told police that she and her mother had been playing hide-and-seek when the fire started. She said she had no idea how the cupboard door came to be locked and she stuck to that throughout the investigation. Of course, there was no way of proving otherwise. The lock just *might* have buckled in the heat. Sally was only ten years old."

"But you thought . . . ?"

"Yes. I thought she did it and so, according to the newspaper librarian, did everyone else. She and her mother were known to have terrible rows."

"How did the fire start?"

"In a pile of kindling wood that was in a basket near the sitting-room fireplace. No kerosene can was ever found but the librarian said one reporter who had covered the story said there was a strong smell of it around the house."

Rachel was silent for a moment, then she said, "Did you know she had left the psychiatric place . . . Rapley?"

"No! If I had, I'd never have left you alone. Just before we were married I phoned the superintendent at Rapley and asked him about Sally. He said she seemed to have improved but it was unlikely that she would ever be well enough to leave."

"Yet she did. She came down here and bought a house and appeared to be absolutely normal! How?"

"If she had gone on improving there was no way they could have kept her."

"And she must have started looking for you."

"It wouldn't have been difficult for her to find me. She only needed a copy of *Bird of Paradise*. Remember the blurb? 'William Chater now lives with his wife, Rachel, in an old rectory near Chichester, Sussex.'"

Rachel sat up suddenly. "Bill! Your book! I found a piece of paper with my dream on it and—and a plan to get rid of an unwanted wife. When Celia told me Sally was in Hollywood, I thought . . ." She stopped.

"That *you* were the unwanted wife?" He began to laugh. "I used that dream of yours as the basis for the plot, but I didn't tell you because I didn't want to say anything at that stage that would remind you of the accident. The book's nearly finished, incidentally; you can read it any time you like."

She felt the last shadows falling from her mind. After a moment she said, "And all the time I was blaming that poor, wretched cat I injured for everything that happened. Alec said Celia kept cats. Is that why you don't like them?"

"Yes. She always had a house full of them. When I left her I never wanted to see another cat." He stretched and glanced toward the window. "My God, it's getting light. It's tomorrow!" He stood up, but she stayed where she was, frowning.

"What is it?"

"Something I'd forgotten to ask. Darling, what made you come back so suddenly?"

"Don't you remember? You wrote me that letter about your trip to London. You mentioned Sally's name for the first time. I was terrified. I tried to call you, but the line was constantly engaged because you'd taken the phone off the hook. Anything else to talk about?"

"No. I expect I'll think of things though. We both will."

"Let's wait until we do." He held out his hand to help her up. "Come on. Bed."

21

A week later Rachel, with Sophie on her knee and Bill beside her, was on the airplane to Los Angeles. The sky was a clear, cloudless blue, and below her the wheat country of Kansas stretched yellow-green to the far horizon.

"What are you thinking about?" Bill said. "Not getting the retrospective shakes, I hope?"

"No. Curiously enough, I was thinking about the good things: red and gold autumn days on the Downs, sitting in front of our fire, knowing Alec . . ."

She stopped, remembering the Alec they had seen the day before leaving England, lying in his hospital bed. He was out of danger and would be able to return to his cottage soon, but he had been a quieter, sadder Alec as he peered at them out of his one remaining, half-blind eye.

"He was in love with Celia," she said. "I don't think he'll ever really get over it."

His neck had still been bandaged, his voice little more than a whisper, but he had insisted on talking as they sat beside him.

"I started to wonder about Celia that day you came and tried so hard to make me understand what you'd been going through, Rachel," he said. "You suspected her, but you didn't know *why*, and at first I just thought you were—not yourself. Then as you were talking I started to remember things. Like the time she pulled up in her car when I was out for a walk. She was coming from the direction of your house, and later I realized it was the day you had found the pillow over Sophie's face. Another thing: the day after Franco died I ran into Moira Renshaw in the village shop and she asked me what had happened—you remember I'd called David from your place. We got talking about Warfarin and she said that David would have to be more careful in future. He kept his Warfarin on a shelf in the big barn where anyone could get hold of it. Then she remarked that only the previous week she had been showing Celia around the farm and she had nearly knocked it off the shelf. When you had gone after our talk, obviously convinced I didn't believe anything you had said, I phoned Moira. She remembered the incident and said that she had explained about Warfarin to Celia, who had been interested and asked her questions about the effect of the poison." He paused and shifted on his pillows.

"I have the feeling that my bloody head will fall off if I move too much," he said wryly. "Where was I? Warfarin. Well, I went up to see David. He hadn't used the poison since he heard about the dog, but we went together and had a look at the tin. It was where it belonged, but he opened it and said he thought there was less in it than there should have been. He couldn't be certain, though. Of course I didn't tell him about my suspicions about Celia. I kept hoping that something would turn up to convince me I was all wrong. Unfortunately, it didn't."

"So Celia laid it down somewhere Franco would get it?" Rachel had said. "It didn't even have to be at the Renshaws. She could have scratched Franco with . . . a brooch, a thorn, anything, then fed him a piece of poisoned meat."

"None of this need have happened," he said wretchedly. "I worked it all out and, as we know now, I was right. But I wouldn't let myself believe it. I *couldn't* believe Celia would do such things. I mean, why should she?"

"That was exactly my question," Rachel said.

Speaking with increasing difficulty, he went on, as though driven by a need to talk it all out of his system. "I suppose that the clincher for me was the dead cat. Originally, when I did the autopsy and found it hadn't been run over, but strangled, I more or less dismissed it from my mind. Maybe because I couldn't bear to face the implication of that, either. I decided that someone must have wanted to get rid of it and had slung the body out from a passing car. It wasn't until your story forced me to think along different lines that I saw what must have happened."

M19

"I believe she was trying to scare me to death," Rachel said. "She piled one horror on another. She knew I hated being in that house alone and she tried to isolate me. She made one mistake, though, and that was when she lied to me about your affair with Mrs. Mason."

"Yes," he said. "Anyone but a stranger like you would have known at once it was a lie."

Now, as California's mountains replaced the plains below them, a memory of the terror returned and she reached for Bill's hand and clutched Sophie more tightly. He seemed to read her mind. "It's okay now," he said softly. "It's all over. She can't ever bother us again."